HERITAGE BUILDERS

THREE
SEARCHING KINGS

FOLLOWING
BETHLEHEM'S STAR

A Historical Novel
by
ELMER TOWNS

HERITAGE BUILDERS PUBLISHING
MONTEREY, CLOVIS CALIFORNIA

HERITAGE BUILDERS PUBLISHING
© 2015

First Edition 2015

Contributing Editors, Kate and Tina Crenshaw
Cover Design, Rae House
Book Design, Nord Compo
Published by Heritage Builders Publishing
Clovis, Monterey California 93619
www.HeritageBuilders.com   1-888-898-9563

ISBN 978-1-942603-00-9

Printed and bound in the United States of America

HERITAGE BUILDERS

TABLE OF CONTENTS

....

INTRODUCTION

....

The story of three searching kings is an historic novel written for your enjoyment and inspiration.

Note the historical facts in the story. Wise men came from the East because they saw His star and brought gifts to worship the Baby-King. "We have seen His star in the East and have come to worship Him" (Matt. 2:2). They asked King Herod in Jerusalem where He could be found. Herod then called Jewish scholars who showed him the prediction from Micah 5:2 that the Messiah would be born in Bethlehem. The star reappeared to the wise men, and they followed it to Bethlehem where they gave the Christ Child their gifts and worshipped Him. Then being warned of God in a dream, they went home another way and didn't tell Herod. As a result of Herod's jealousy and neurotic fears, he sent soldiers to slaughter all the children in Bethlehem two years old and younger.

I have added people and events to the story to help you understand what might have happened. The servant to the wise men was named Jewel. You'll have to guess who he might be. Jewel adds information about Bible prophecy, asks questions to direct the wise men, then reinforces them in their journey to Jerusalem.

Of all the things that happened to the Christ Child, why was the story of the wise men included in the Bible? Perhaps God wanted to explain where money came from for Joseph and Mary to live a couple of years in Egypt. Also, perhaps God wanted to focus on Gentiles (the wise men) who worshipped Jesus, which was predictive of the Gentile church that would champion the cause of Jesus after the Jews rejected Him.

Don't miss the last chapter; it tells of a university professor lecturing students regarding the various questions about the wise men that have puzzled Christian scholars since the birth of Christ. This section has footnotes for further study and will help you understand why I have interpreted the story as I have.

- How many wise men were there?
- Were they kings?
- What was the star?
- Who saw the star?
- Why were they directed to Bethlehem?
- What different way did they return home?
- Did one of the twelve apostles actually baptize them?
- Where were they buried?
- Then for your own inquiry, how were Jewel and the professor similar?

Read carefully to see how three "kings" search to find the baby Jesus, then worship Him with their lives and treasures. In turn, Christ touches them and changes their lives forever.

At the top of Liberty Mountain
Lynchburg, VA

ELMER L. TOWNS
2015

1

SAVED FROM SLAVERY

....

Three Wise Men—Born into Kingly Lives—Become Friends

Muscles bulged from under his body armor. With a snap of his wrist he snatched a horsefly from off the horn of his saddle, then he squeezed its life slowly away. The Commander of the guard sat arrogantly upon his gleaming white stallion. The crowd squirmed out of the way as the Commander led his soldiers toward the agora, the marketplace where the auctioneer would sell off the slaves, some captured warriors, others just captured victims. They were chained in a column, but each kept pace by the vindictive Persian whip.

The noisy market in Narhet attracted buyers from all over the desert plains of Persia. However, today the crowd silenced itself lest any angered the Commander or his henchmen— soldiers. The clanking of the bronze leg shackles on the slaves penetrated the self-imposed silence.

The Commander was darker skinned than most Persians. *"Probably a half breed,"* Melchior thought to himself. Melchior, a magian, watched the parade of human merchandise with calculated insight. He could almost tell the nationality of each slave by his cultural distinctiveness.

The huge white stallion bumped Melchior out of the way as the Commander rode past, neither arrogant man willing to step out of the way of the other.

The Commander was short by army size, unusual because an army leader had to demonstrate *might makes right*. His soldiers had to fear him to follow him. Melchior thought again,

"Little men overcome their introversive stature by arrogance and dictatorial strength."

The merciless Persian sun punished all standing in its brilliance. Melchior surveyed the human merchandise for sale in the slave market. He had no pity for any of the human chattel. He didn't need a house slave; he had a Hebrew slave, at least he thought Jewel was a Hebrew slave. Jewel spoke ancient *Hebrew,* "the language beyond the river."

Melchior was old by the count of children, but his step was spry. His long grey beard—well manicured—and his stringy hair that grew from under his bright green three-cornered hat identified him as a magi.

To call a man a magian was to reverence his caste; they were followers of Zoroastrianism, known for their wisdom and many languages. The magi had ruled Persia 400 years ago, before their leader was murdered, and magi became a minor influence in the nation. The common people hated the "religious" rule of the magi. When saying magi, they spit for the very thought of magi left a foul taste of meaningless moral laws in their mouths.

"Magi think they are better than everyone else," some complained.

"That's because we are." The magi would end the conversation with the self-assurance they were God-ordained to brilliance. And in conceit they would begin speaking an unknown tongue when talking to a commoner, then switch to a second or third language in the same conversation to demonstrate their erudition.

Why would they do that? Because magi didn't lower themselves to speak to commoners. They arrogantly taught the ignorant what they needed to know.

Melchior viewed the two dozen slaves forced to stand

in the scorching sun—their hands tied with stretched leather, their feet shackled with bronze. Melchior thought of the childish proverb taught children, *"The Persian sun only burns the outer skin, but its rays kill the inner man."*

These slaves were herded by Parthian soldiers. The light in the soldiers' eyes told Melchior that soon they would get their pay for successfully herding human chattel. Soldiers kept half of the sale price for slaves; the other price went to the kingdom.

By the looks of these slaves, they were captured from the Romans who controlled the other side of the Euphrates River. Usually, slaves were transported a long distance from home to help remove any temptation to run away and return home.

"Take off the leg shackles." The booming voice of the Commander surprised Melchior. He thought, *Such a big voice for a little man.*

The bronze chains rattled as they fell to the dust, but the hands of each slave were still tied tightly. A Parthian soldier bound a slave with wet leather thongs. Leather stretches when wet, but shrinks when dry. Therefore, their swollen wrists were bound so tightly that the circulation of blood was often cut off, producing agonizing pain. The slaves struggled to keep their leather bindings wet by constantly rubbing them on their perspiring bodies.

Melchior then spied a prisoner with the appearance of wealth; the beard was trimmed neatly and the hair around his eyes had been edged. His fingernails gave evidence of care and were manicured, although now dirty. Melchior thought to himself, *This man is educated; he is not used to manual work.*

"Who are you?" Melchior addressed a middle-aged black man in the Persian language. At first the black man showed defiance; he jerked away, turning his head away from Melchior.

"Who are you?" Melchior again demanded, but this time in Latin.

The black man jerked around to glare at his questioning.

He recognized the erudition of Melchior, so he answered in Greek, "I am Balthazar from Ethiopia. I am the son of the king of my tribe. I have been educated under my nation's finest teachers."

"Ah, I see you speak Persian . . . Latin . . . Greek . . . but do you also speak Aramanean, the tribal language of the commoners?"

"Yes," he answered in Aramanean.

"And do you speak and read Hebrew?" Melchior thought this man who calls himself Balthazar might help him in his current research of the sacred Hebrew text.

"Why do you ask if I read Hebrew?"

Melchior wanted to know how broadly educated was this black man from Ethiopia, this black man who stood erect like a king. When Balthazar walked, he didn't slouch as a slave; he marched liked a general reviewing his troops.

The Parthians had captured this muscular black man from the Romans, but Balthazar's self-imposed dignity intimidated his captors. The more they ripped his back with scourges, the taller he stood in their presence.

Suddenly the thought hit Melchior, *This black man has the qualities of a magian; he has the power of the gods upon him. I can train him to be one of us.* He yelled out to the soldiers,

"RELEASE THIS MAN," Melchior pointed to the black man, "he's a MAGIAN . . . he has the power of the stars."

The magi were a sacred caste of the Medes: priests of Zoroastrianism. The kings who ruled the Media-Persian Empire revered the magi and sought their counsel. Yet, the magi were hated because they used their intellect and power to rule all they surveyed. Cyrus the Persian emperor who conquered the known world did so because he conquered the political power of the magi.

Eventually the magi revolted and set up Gaumata as their king over Persian. Gaumata was a magian and ruled as 60th magi and king. But Gaumata was murdered. Then Darius became king.

This is the Darius who threw Daniel in the lion's den. This story was legend in Persia even in that day.

Melchior became teary eyed when the name Gaumata was spoken; this was his grandfather twelve generations ago. Melchior had kingly blood running in his veins, but his family had not ruled for twelve generations.

When magi demanded, soldiers would not interfere. The word *magi* meant magic to them. They were afraid of the magis' black magic. When magi commanded, soldiers might not obey them, but they wouldn't get involved.

"RELEASE THIS MAN NOW!" Melchior's bold, authoritarian voice rang out over the marketplace. The old stooped-shouldered magian commanded what he wanted. Soldiers feared an evil curse from magi, but at the same time detested them for their intrusion into governmental affairs.

Melchior marched up to a quivering soldier and pulled his sword from his belt. The soldier did not deny him, but fell to the ground with arms shielding his head as though Melchior would decapitate him.

"NOT YOU . . .," Melchior pointed to Balthazar, "HIM!"

The charade was working. Not a soldier stopped Melchior; Commander looked on in disgust from astride his white stallion.

Melchior raised the sword over Balthazar's head, "If the magi can't have him, shall I kill him now?"

Balthazar's black eyes were defiant.

No one moved; the soldiers stood statuesquely still. The only thing that moved among the prisoners was their eyes. With wide-eyed anticipation, the soldiers watched Melchior's quick slash of the commandeered sword.

"SLASH!" The leather thongs fell off Balthazar's arms, and he lifted both arms in victory.

The prisoners cheered carefully, not loudly, but cheered quickly, then fell silent. Their eyes darted again to their captives— the soldiers. The military held attention; no one moved.

Commander on the great, white horse smiled slyly, but not so anyone noticed. His small, beady black eyes did not move from Melchior.

"COME WITH ME TO THE MAGIS' CHANTRY." Melchior pointed to the dusty road that led to freedom for Balthazar.

But Balthazar didn't move; neither did any of the prisoners. In like manner, the soldiers held their solitary attention; none flinched.

"COME," Melchior commanded. "NOW!"

"NO!"

Balthazar's single word shocked the audience. Here the black man was offered freedom. Was this man's arrogance turning down the sanctuary of the magis' chantry?

Slowly the black man's finger pointed to the rear of the prisoners. Every cautious eye of the soldiers followed the massive pointing finger. Then, too, every lustful eye of every prisoner followed the black finger as it moved to a prisoner whose skin was lighter in contrast to the black hand that was pointing him out. He pointed to a white man. The bombastic Ethiopian voice rang out over the crowd,

"HE MUST GO WITH US."

"Why?" the lone voice of his savior, Melchior, asked in unbelief. "WHY HIM . . .?"

Balthazar spoke in Latin to the fair-skinned prisoner. He walked to where the gaunt, light-skinned young man stood. "Do you know the stars?"

"*Ito vero,*" they all heard the man answer.

Again Balthazar spoke, but this time in Greek, "Do you understand the gods who live in the Parthenon or the Acropolis in Athens?"

"*Neh,*" he spoke Greek.

A third time was not too much for Balthazar. He again asked the young white-faced prisoner, "Have you been to the

Nile? Have you seen the sphinx and the pyramids . . . and can you read the inscriptions on the tombs of the pharaohs?"

"*Aiwa*, the secret of their hearts are hidden in my heart," he said in Egyptian dialect.

A fourth time Balthazar's voice rang out over the swelling crowd, "Do you know the secrets of Jehovah, God of the Jews, THE LORD who slaughtered his enemies the Egyptians?"

"*Ken* . . ., I can speak and read their sacred Scriptures, and I know the secrets hidden in their Torah."

Then Balthazar put his freedom on the line. He asked Melchior—a man he just met— "Cut this man loose and take him with us." Before the old Persian magian could answer, Gaspar, the white prisoner, spoke,

"The three of us will be three magi. We magi know the three stars in the belt of Orion that point to Sirius are called the three kings. Sirius is called the star of the East. That star is the Dayspring. Once a year—every 25th day of the 12th month—the stars of the three kings rise at the same point on the horizon as the sun. When the sun is perpendicular with the earth, the one King of heaven will bring peace to earth."

The audience of ignorant slaves and soldiers recognized they were learning in the presence of a magian. These three men were trained in astrology, they knew the stars, and understood the mysteries of life. Again Gaspar broke the silence—pleading his case for freedom.

"The people you hate, I hate; the Romans have spilled the blood of our fathers and mothers, our brothers and sisters. I, too, was to be a king—just like Balthazar and just like Melchior. We are kings denied."

The soldiers had heard many prisoners lie—all types of lies—to barter their freedom. Melchior did not know if he should move toward the young white man to also free him. All thought Gaspar's speech was down payment to liberty. The moment was tense. Could Melchior pull it off? He glanced over to the Commander, still sitting smugly on his white charger.

"Here . . ." Gaspar, the white-skin-slave pulled out from his dirtied tunic a worn and torn scroll. Holding it high for all to see, he announced, "This is a copy of a scroll written by Isaiah the Hebrew prophet, a man who did miracles; he could pray so that old men became young again."

Gaspar continued, "This scroll tells when the King of the universe will come to give us peace." Then, to make his point, Gasper proclaimed, "When the King comes, the lion and lamb will lie together in peace. The vultures will not sweep down on its prey, and men will no longer lie and steal."

"*STOP!*" Commander's shout stopped everything about the unfolding scene.

"NO!"

Commander's small frame slipped off his mount with no effort of hands or feet. His body was one with his animal, and he slipped effortlessly to the ground. He landed with no sound.

"**NO!** . . .," Commander's loud voice froze the crowd.

"No . . . you will not cut the leather binding from my prisoners." He walked menacingly toward Melchior and the prisoner holding the scroll.

As the captain approached, he slowly pulled his sword from its sash. The sight of the curved sword sliding from its resting place frightened the crowd . . . the soldiers, the slaves, and Melchior. The Persians believe, *never awaken a sword in anger, unless it draws blood from its victim.*

The sword was pulled; was it an angry sword? Whose blood would it taste? Melchior had been courageous up to this point. Now the old magian had doubts. Had he pushed the military beyond patience? Melchior knew the animosity between the magian and those who served the king. Would the unleashed sword sing his funeral ode?

Melchior nervously fingered the sword he was holding,

knowing he was no match for the advancing Commander. If he dropped his sword, captains were known to cut in pieces those who surrender. If he turned and ran, he could never come back to the marketplace.

The crowd stood erect, standing on tip-toes. The bourgeois loved to see blood spilled, and this seemed to be the best moment to satisfy their appetite for execution.

Commander looked up to the taller Melchior, then into the frightened face of scared Gaspar. He lifted his sword in defiance.

In one swift, meticulous slice of his sword, Commander cut the leather thongs off Gasper, the European slave. And in that slice, he was offering the surprised slave his freedom. Then the captain put his mouth to whisper in Melchior's ear, "My father was a Magian; I am from the line of Gaumata." He smiled and added, "No one must know."

The soldiers began moving slowly away, leaving two prisoners separated from the rest, but still surrounded by a circle of humanity. The three men had attracted the focus of heaven— Melchior, Balthazar, and Gasper—three avarice magi who had been denied their kingly heritage.

The three walked to the edge of town to the chantry, the facilities where magi lived. This home was built in a circle; no other house in town was built round like a wheel, but Melchior's home was like a continuous circle, his view of life.

2

SETTLING INTO THE CHANTRY

....

Each Grieving Why He's not A King

Melchior showed the two former slaves around his chantry. Melchior pointed to the room where Jewel slept, commenting, "The servants sleep in there."

"I'm not your SLAVE," Balthazar raised his voice sarcastically. Given the fact the black Ethiopian had just been freed from captivity, there was no sign of gratitude, only continued defiance.

"I may have had chains, but I'm a free man inside." He continued his belligerence, "I choose the one I'll serve, and I'll choose the orders I'll obey."

Melchior's eyebrow lifted; he said nothing. The wise old scholar decided to study the cultural clash of his black guest and not react emotionally. Melchior displayed the near eastern quality of inscrutable mystery while Balthazar showed African spontaneous emotionalism. Their cultures would clash again in the future.

The incompatible threesome sat in a shaded garden in the rear of the chantry. Jewel served each one a cup of hot dark liquid.

"Astonishing . . .," laughed Balthazar, laughing at no one in particular, then announced, "Astonishing . . . your slave has served us in three different cups, and he served me in a cup carved from stone, the type of cup we Ethiopians used back home."

Gasper hadn't said much to this point, but agreed, "I'm

also astonished . . . the slave has served me in a thick clay mug, the kind used back in Tarshish."

Melchior, rebuking his guest in his new eastern demeanor, said softly, "We magi don't call a man a slave; that reminds him of his chains. Jewel is not a slave; he's a servant. He is a free man who has chosen this position. He can leave anytime he chooses."

The silence of the two accepted the rebuke. Then Melchior smiled, "His name is Jewel, like a gem hidden in the earth; it's beauty is not seen until it is polished." Then Melchior told Jewel, "Your tea is magnificent."

When Jewel left their presence, Melchior added, "Polish this jewel and its beauty will enhance your dignity. If you treat him harshly, you scratch the surface and a defaced jewel never shines as brightly again." Then he added, "When your jewel loses value in your sight, you also lose your value in your own perception."

Silence—the lecture settled in.

"One main thing," Melchior added, "every time you thank him—loquaciously—you raise the bar for him to do a better job next time."

Again, silence.

"This is the way the magi kings treat their servants," Melchior explained. He told his new friends that his grandfather—twelve generations ago—was the magi-king who ruled the Persian Kingdom after Cyrus and before Darius and Xerxes. Melchior told how the magi-king ruled until his ancient grandfather was assassinated—murdered—in his sleep.

"One day the magi will rule again, and perhaps I shall be king."

Both Balthazar listened to their host until he added why he would be king. What he said piqued their attention.

"I will rule again, for the stars predict a coming king will rule in peace—magi-peace.

When Melchior said *stars*, he said something both men believed, but each believed it for a different reason.

The magi brotherhood will return . . .

"Ha . . .," Balthazar interrupted his host. "We in Ethiopia have learned that evil lurks in the kindest men, and given an opportunity, evil will drip from his heart in a lie . . . or a thought . . . or a murder. Evil is an open sore that will not heal; it's a disease in the heart of each individual. If you do not keep your hand upon the head of a slave, when given the opportunity, the slave will rise up to be king and you will be his slave."

Then Balthazar in his deep African voice told how he came from a line of kings. His father had many slaves. He fed them well, gave them a place to sleep, but he had taskmasters to make them work. The Ethiopian smiled as he opined,

"Sleep seeks every man to join him, and rest begs every slave to stop their work and join him."

"No . . .," Balthazar did not agree with his Persian host. "My father worked his slaves hard, and when I become king—for I will go home—I will work my slaves hard."

Balthazar's dark black eyes narrowed as he explained how the Roman legions invaded Ethiopia. The Ethiopian soldiers were larger and more fierce in battle, but the Romans defeated them. While there were many more black soldiers than Romans, the Romans were victorious, proving discipline trumps enthusiasm, and obedience wins over brute strength.

"The Romans put my family in chains, then spread us throughout the empire. I've not seen a relative of mine since I was taken from Ethiopia in chains. The Romans are careful to send each slave a long way from home so they are not tempted to run away home.

"The Romans sent me to a small out-of-the-way village in Syria. While there, the Parthians attacked the Romans."

He explained the Parthians hated the Romans. "Did the Parthians release me? No! I thought they would be my brothers because we both hated the Romans. But hate does not make brotherhood. Hate makes one man chain his brother. So the Parthians brought me to Persia in chains—Roman chains I might add. They did not even have the dignity to put Parthian chains on me.

Then Balthazar said to Melchior, "Your claim of kingship goes back twelve generations. That's twelve generations of people you barely know. My father was killed by the Romans three years ago. I could have been king, but no, I'm a king in chains."

Balthazar looked around the room as though appealing for sympathy, but none was given. Melchior and Gasper had their own wounds. Then Balthazar concluded, "What kind of king has no subjects, no scepter, and no crown?"

Then he answered his own question, "Only a self-deceived man calls himself king when he has no power—nothing."

The wearisome triad had been sitting quietly for almost an hour, each man immersed in his own lost dreams. Melchior and Balthazar had confessed their ill-fated past, and now they were silently rehashing the "what-ifs" of history.

Each in his own way asked, "What would have happened if . . .?"

But the question doesn't dig anyone out of a hole; it only makes the hole of bitterness deeper. It only makes it harder to forget the past and live for the future.

"Gentlemen . . .," Gasper broke the silence to announce, "you are proud of your family line. You have delicious memories of what might have been.

"I was the oldest son of a Gaelic king on the border of the countries of Tartaris and Gaul. My mother was a hot-blooded woman of Spanish descent, married to a weak, vacillating Frenchman who reigned from a castle high above the Mediterranean shoreline. I was his first son.

"My mother was really the king because my father did what my mother demanded. She screamed, and she lied . . .

She plotted . . . and she flirted with all in my father's court who possessed what she wanted—power.

"My mother hated me from conception, claiming my father raped her. My mother detested me because of hard labor pains, and she refused me breast milk.

"My mother loved my little brother and planned for him to be king in my place. She made us play a game of cards, then she made me gamble my family crest ring. She cheated for my brother to win the family crest and the throne.

"My father said I'd be the next king no matter who won the card game. My mother plotted to put my brother on the throne. One night I was kidnapped from my bed, rowed by skiff to a Roman galleon anchored in our small harbor and sold as a slave to the Romans.

"The Romans told me my captors took my prized cape given to me by my father and covered it with blood to convince my father that I was dead. They let him believe a wild animal had killed me while I was hunting. Then my younger brother would be the next king."

"Yes, Balthazar, you're right," Gasper concluded his story, "the Romans shipped their slaves far from home so they wouldn't be tempted to return. But I made fools of them—I hated my family and I detested my home. I'll never return there again."

As the three magi walked past a heavy door leading to the Circle Room in the center of the house, Melchior remarked almost innocently, "No one is allowed in that room; it is my private oasis. I go there to renew my mind and soul."

"Why can't we just look in?" Balthazar bluntly asked.

"Because it's private to me," Melchior answered just as bluntly. "Everyone has an intimate part of his life that he doesn't share with the world. That's my secret privilege."

Balthazar didn't say any more out loud, but all types of

thoughts ran through his head. *Are their dead corpses in there?* And, *What crime is he hiding?*

At the same time Gaspar's thoughts followed a different flow. *We can't be intimate friends when Melchior keeps secrets. Perhaps with time I'll be invited into the Circle Room.*

Jewel had been listening to all three telling of their desire to be king. He also recognized the embarrassment of the moment. Being an obedient servant, Jewel stepped meekly into the conversation to apologize. "I listened to your conversations so I can know you better—to serve you better."

Jewel dropped the subject of the Circle Room, then added, "I serve the LORD God who created man in the beginning. The LORD puts desires in the hearts of all men, and it is no coincidence that all three of you were only a heartbeat away from the throne."

The three listened attentively to Jewel's explanation. The servant continued, "The LORD has a wonderful plan for each of us, yet He watches to see how we control our destiny."

Then Jewel came to the point he was making. "My God is powerful enough to plan the circumstances of life. He has given you three a passion to be king, so you could help prepare His Son to sit upon the throne of Israel and eventually rule over the earth."

The three would-be kings didn't debate Jewel; they allowed him his religious beliefs. Who knows, Jewel might worship the true God of gods. And if Jewel was right, they might one day worship the true God of heaven. Jewel thought to himself,

"Maybe those three men understand the attraction of the throne. Maybe these three can become king-makers. What can be better than being a king? These three might help the world recognize the coming King of all kings."

3

THE STAR NOT DENIED

....

One Night Changed Their Lives

It was the 25th day of the 12th month. The three meditative kings were silently gazing into the cloudless night sky. The stars seemed more brilliant than usual. The three magi were carefully studying their instruments to observe the phenomena of the three king's star.

Then Melchior broke the silence, "The three belt stars of Orion are pointing to Sirius—the star of the east. At this time of year all three come up over the eastern horizon at the identical spot as the sun.

"Yes, there they are," Gaspar whispered a shout. "Behold the Dayspring from on high. These stars spring over the eastern horizon from the same point as the sun."

"In Africa we teach it's the anointing event," the deep, resonant voice of Balthazar whispered. "It announces that a new Baby-King is born, or a young man is crowned king. It's when the son of the father is ready to make his entrance known to all."

"Does it mean a king is born this day?" Then Balthazar thought, *Did I really ask that?*

The eyes of Melchior and Gasper met. They knew what Balthazar was thinking, *Three earthly kings introducing the King from heaven.*

Jewel's sandals were heard scraping on the sandy steps

outside the building. He was bringing evening tea to warm the innards in a chilly evening breeze. Jewel announced,

"Tea changes everything". With tea they could discuss politics . . . or family . . . or their aches and pains . . . or the students who would one day take their place."

Jewel knew what they had been discussing, or thinking. Jewel thought, *On this day a Baby-King would be born among the Jews. The Child-King would command nature and would be obeyed. He would command the people of the world, and He would be obeyed. The Child-King would be a Jew, born among Jews, the King of the Jews.*

"Is today the day?" Balthazar asked, "or will the King be born next year?"

"Or the following year after that?" questioned Melchior.

"Or the year after that?" added Gaspar.

"Look!" Jewel whispered loudly in reverence of the magi's presence. "Look . . . coming from the west!"

Jewel was the first to see it—or did he know something and call attention to the new star? A brilliant light exploded on the horizon, sparkling and dancing its way to earth. Transfixed . . . the three magi and Jewel couldn't take their eyes off the glory they saw. They were shocked into silence. Muted, they stared at a phenomenon never seen in Persia. The brightest star in the world sprang up in the western sky; it didn't arise in the east as all other stars.

The glistening star grew bigger as clouds tumbled over one another. Were they seeing illuminated smoke in the sky? Or were they seeing clouds 1,000 miles away that intermittently covered the light, but only briefly? Was the star flashing its rays to attract attention?

"That star has many lights within one light," Melchior whispered. He was afraid to speak loudly or shout. The light might go away.

"The star seems to shine downward to the earth," Gasper added. "That star is not shining upwards . . . or to the horizon, but its beam is focused in one direction."

Silence gripped the three magi and Jewel. They were afraid their words would interfere with their memory of what they saw. Men are silent when they don't know what to say. Perhaps they realize anything said will embarrass them later.

"Where's the star heading?" Melchior asked. He knew the answer, but didn't want to say. Melchior knew if he said what he thought, he would be considered illogical . . . crazy . . . or naive. *The star is going the wrong way*, he thought.

Stars come over the eastern horizon—the same as the sun and moon—and set in the western horizon. But this light seemed to have arisen in the west . . . now it was climbing in the dark sky. The star was going the wrong way.

"Is this the end of the world? Never has a star gone backward!" Gasper spit out his words of apocalyptic fear.

"Or is it the beginning of a new world?" answered Balthazar. "This could be a new genesis." Then Balthazar asked a rhetorical question to no one in particular, "Is God starting a new order? Could it be the world is burning up and the fire will eventually reach us?"

The three kings retreated to their couches. They had special beds built so they could lie for hours looking into the dark heavens. But they were not concerned with the darkness; it was rays from the new star that intrigued them. If they could interrupt the light of this new star, they might understand God.

"What I see is not a natural stellar phenomenon," remarked Melchior. "All I know for sure . . . is that what I see I've never seen before."

"Nor has anyone else," responded Balthazar.

Gasper analyzed, "Jupiter—the royal star—and Saturn have come together in the past several months. Perhaps they are coming together with another planet, a star we don't know about?"

"No . . . !" Balthazar quickly corrected. "They are in the wrong place in the sky."

"Why is it going the wrong direction?" Melchior asked, thus ending that speculation.

"It may be an *asteroid* or a comet that we suddenly see flying toward our earth," was the next suggestion Gasper made. The three magi didn't answer the rhetorical question, as it wasn't a question, but a statement. Maybe the light they saw was the first appearance of a comet whose orbit thrust it into sight. If it was a comet . . .

"Will it get brighter each evening?"

"We will know within a week or month if it's a comet."

Each of the three thought of the 76-year comet. Every seventy-six years a comet streaked across the sky, dancing on its tail. The astronomers could see the comet for a short while—short when compared to seventy-six years. Then it would streak away to return again in seven decades.

The three astronomer-magis thought themselves fortunate to have seen the seventy-six year comet in their lifetime. Many had not seen it once; none had seen it twice.

"Is that an occultation, an eclipse of Jupiter with the moon that's come early this year?" Gasper was the most analytical one of the three; he reasoned out everything.

"No," answered Melchior, "the occultation comes in April." The old man summarized, "Besides, we see the moon in the East; this light is in the West."

"I have heard about super novas," Melchior shared with his friends. "I have not seen one, but the ancient magi tell about them, and I've read about them." Melchior explained a super nova was an explosive event where a star erupts and explodes, giving off dazzling planetary light. Perhaps we are seeing a super nova that has erupted? Perhaps it is bigger than any previous.

"What we know about super novas," explained Melchior "is that they don't explode on schedule." He explained that when gasses reach a high compression, or boiling point, they explode.

The three magi continued watching the bright light on the western horizon. They were convinced it was not a conjugation of planets, nor was it a comet. Everything about this light was mysterious.

"But could we be seeing the brilliance of a *stellar nova* which suddenly increases in brilliance, then fades away?"

"But nothing arises in the west and travels to the east," again the doubtful Gasper said.

Then the Ethiopian broke the reflective mood,

"I must say what I am thinking. Something this magnificent, from such a long way away, may be supernatural. It may be a light from God . . ." his words trailed off.

"Or it is God Himself . . .?"

Gasper, the one who brought the Isaiah manuscript to the chantry, suggested the answer could be found in his scroll. "I remember reading that Isaiah said, 'The people that walk in darkness, will see a great light. The light will shine on them that dwell in the shadow of darkness'" (Isaiah 9: 2). Then Gasper asked, "Is this light coming from Galilee, the northern section of the Jews' Holy Land?"

Balthazar pointed west toward the Holy Land. "The light is coming from that direction. Did Isaiah mean the light would be their understanding, or would light be like the sun?"

No one answered his question.

Then Balthazar continued on a topic, "If the light is God Himself, then it's the light we read about in the books of Moses. We may be seeing the Shekinah brightness of God." He went on to explain that the pillar of fire by night and the pillar of smoke by day led Israel through the wilderness. It was the presence of God Who stood in the camp by night to protect them.

Melchior and Gasper both shook their heads in agreement. There was no natural explanation for the great star they saw in the West.

The three magi lay on their observation couches all evening. They didn't know what would happen. They refused to leave – even look away – afraid they would miss something extraordinary, something supernatural.

As the sun peaked over the eastern horizon, the star in the west began to fade. Then like all the night stars, they disappeared in the glare of the sun. They don't go away; they just can't be seen. The three magi sat on their couches until it was full dawn, and they no longer saw the star.

The following day the three magi visited a chantry some distance away. They arrived in the early afternoon and shared lunch. The receiving magi could tell their three comrades had come to ask a question, but didn't ask the three why they came or what it was they wanted. They waited.

Finally, Melchior, the aged one, asked, "Were you watching the stars last night?"

"Yes."

"Did you look to the eastern horizon only, or did you look west?"

"We looked both ways."

"Did you see anything unusual in the sky last night?"

"Nothing unusual."

"Did you see a star arise from the western horizon?"

There were snickers among the hosts. Everyone knew that stars don't come up from the western horizon. The ancient magi—the host leader of the chantry—sarcastically suggested,

"If you suddenly saw a star in the west, but it descended behind the western horizon," he let his question sink in, "maybe you were dizzy, and you thought it descended over the western horizon?"

Balthazar glared at him in defiance as though he were

being treated as a child. Melchior and Gasper only smiled as those who knew better.

Later that evening they sat quietly on the roof top as the cool winter evening washed away the daylight, as water washes dust from a table top. Each man was deep in thought about what they saw yester evening—the brilliant light in the West. Each man knew what he saw; each knew it was, perhaps, the brightest star he had ever seen.

Each wanted to discuss with the others why other magi had not seen the light. Why had star-gazers they visited that afternoon not seen the dazzling star they saw? Each was coming to the conclusion that God had shown the star to them, but no one else.

Are we unique in the universe that God would seek us out? Gasper thought inwardly.

Melchior thought about his charts of the heavens that were locked away in the Circle Room. When he had time to retreat to the Circle Room, the wise old magi felt the secrets locked up in that innermost room would help them unlock the secret of the spectacular star.

When the mood became silent among the three magi, Jewel knew it was time for some relaxation. He smiled, then entered the room carrying a tray and cups, the favorite cup for each magian. Steam floated upwards in small circles.

"Hot tea anyone?"

4

THE HEAVENS, BRIGHTER THAN A STAR

Shepherds Near Bethlehem

His was a hard face. The face of a shepherd is hardened with searing heat . . . killing cold . . . extreme weather. His grizzled beard had been hacked off with a dull knife by hands that didn't care to have a handsome face. "The breeze has died down," the older shepherd whispered to his younger companion, keeping his voice down so as not to frighten the sheep they were tending by night. They were shepherds in a field near Bethlehem—in the Holy Land.

"No storms tonight . . . not a cloud on the horizon." The young shepherd glanced from the eastern sky to the west with distrusting eyes. The moon was a bowl of milk, full and clear. The young man was unmoved by the beauty of nature about him. He thirsted for something, but he didn't know what.

The snapping fire burned low, red coals still warming their bare feet. The shepherds had taken shelter from the wind among low, flat limestone rocks, where they built a fire down in a small pit concealed from the breeze. Under the larger rocks the dirt had washed away, leaving shallow caves that afforded the shepherds some protection from the elements. Several shepherds in the largest cave were already wrapped in their tunics . . . sleeping, waiting for their watch.

"Nothing happens this early in the evening," the younger

shepherd moaned, complaining again about his assignment to the early watch. His body was cold, his mind was numb, his world was not empathetic. Everything warm in life had been snatched from him.

"When nothing happens," the older-looking shepherd said impatiently, "maybe then we'll have peace." The older shepherd had lost his faith in God. The only thing he believed in was the tyranny of Rome. He believed in the Roman sword because its sharp edge was his teacher. He believed in the Roman scourge because he had experienced its punishment. But he hated what he believed. He hated Roman taxes and Roman laws. He was filled with revulsion at the sight of every Roman soldier.

"When the Deliverer—the Son of David—comes, we'll have peace," said the younger man. Despite his circumstances, the flame of faith still flickered within him.

"Ha!" snorted the older shepherd. His faith in life and the future had gone out.

Then derisively he spit out the words, "Yes, when the *Deliverer* comes, I can go home . . . rather than hide up here in the hills."

He was but a young man. Hardened by years of running from the Roman authorities, he had finally taken work as a shepherd to hide in obscurity from the soldiers. *If—when the Messiah comes*, he thought almost wanting to believe, *I'll go home.*

The younger shepherd was lost in his own thoughts. He still believed in God. He had prayed for God to send the Messiah, but for a different reason from that of his companion. He had sinned deeply against his family, against his village, against God.

"When the Savior is come," the young man broke the silence, "He will purify my memory."

"What is *that* supposed to mean?" the older voice barked, "He will purify my memory."

"I've done something," the young man confessed. "I try to forget, but I can't."

The young shepherd told his story, some of which his older companion knew, but much of it was unfamiliar and took him by surprise. The younger man had tried many things to eradicate his past, but the memory of his deeds relentlessly pursued him, like a hungry wolf stalking a lost sheep. The young man had worked as a soldier, a camel driver, and shepherd. He had even associated with a band of thieves for a while, but everywhere his sin dogged him.

A warm wind flushed the shepherds' faces, whipping their tunics in the breeze. The older shepherd, who had found himself caught up unexpectedly in his young friend's tale, now found himself puzzled by the sudden, unseasonable heat.

Suddenly, a sparkling light fell on them, as though a blanket of stars had dropped out of heaven. The glistening light blinded the two shepherds. Their eyes burned like a sandstorm, irritating their sight. They covered their heads with their tunics and hid their faces.

Then the night exploded in LIGHT! Blinding light!

Light from the heavens obliterated the darkness, blinding the two shepherds keeping watch over the flocks. With their hearts in their throats and a blinding light stinging their eyes, the shepherds covered their heads with their tunics and hid their faces from the brilliance around them.

The dazzling light pierced the closed eyelids of the sleeping shepherds. Even those in the deeper caves couldn't escape its radiance. It was as though a blanket of a thousand suns had dropped out of heaven and ignited the rocky outcropping. Fear choked the shepherd band like an executioner's hands. Their tongues were mute; their hands paralyzed.

"Do not be afraid," came a voice from the other side of the light.

"Wh-wh-what is it?" the young shepherd finally managed to ask.

"The voice is from heaven. Only heaven can be this bright," said the older shepherd.

As their eyes began to adjust, the younger shepherd shouted, "I see people in the sky. Great crowds of shining people . . . hundreds . . . thousands."

The older man squinted toward the heavens. The glorious light penetrated a breach in the night sky. It flooded through an opening in the sky. The two shepherds saw thousands upon thousands of angels. And they were singing.

"Look . . ., Look . . .!"

All the younger shepherds forced their eyes to look. For most of them looking was painful—like looking directly into the sun.

"There are so many I can't count them," the youth cried. "There are hundreds . . . thousands . . . millions."

"Do not be afraid," the voice behind the light repeated. "I have come to bring you good tidings of great joy to all men." The shepherds exchanged glances.

"Your Savior *was* born tonight in Bethlehem. He is Christ the Lord," the angel proclaimed. "You will find a baby wrapped in cloths, sleeping in a manger in a stable behind an inn."

The younger shepherd glanced again at the old shepherd when he heard the word "Savior." The older shepherd *was* thinking, *Can a child so poor that he sleeps in a feed trough deliver us from Rome? Is this child capable of driving the centurions from our shores?*

Then a magnificent sound flooded the night—the loudest thing they had ever heard, yet a harmonious sound that flooded out the noise of past failures. They tasted music that had never been enjoyed by humans—music far superior to the Levitical singer in the Temple, and a thousand times more beautiful.

The great company of the heavenly host praised God, singing:

"Glory to God in the highest,
And on earth peace, goodwill toward men!"

Then just as suddenly as the angels came, they were gone. Almost *immediately* the nippy winter night dosed on the shepherds, like the chilly darkness that floods an area when a warm fire is extinguished. The older shepherd tugged at his tunic to block the chill.

"Let's go!" The younger shepherd leaped to his feet, waving his arms for everyone to get up. *"Let's go now!"*

"Where?" one of the shepherds asked, unsure whether he might still be asleep and dreaming, albeit more spectacularly than usual.

"Bethlehem!" the young man shouted arid laughed. "Didn't you hear? The Savior is in the stable at an inn in Bethlehem."

The shepherds began to stir, but slowly. They had seen the light and heard the angel. They were in shock ... their senses singed. They didn't know how to react.

The shepherd in charge was now fully awake. He thought about what he had heard and about all they had experienced. He had been sleeping when the light first fell upon them. When awakened, he had known instinctively this was not sunrise. He had somehow known the light was heaven coming down to earth. He now spoke up. "If the Baby is the Savior," the head shepherd instructed the group, "we must bring the Savior an offering."

The head shepherd understood that sinners were to bring a gift to God when seeking salvation. He had sold many lambs to worshipers, and he had come to recognize a look in the eyes of those who truly wanted salvation. He saw this look now in the eyes of the young shepherd and the men around him. If the Savior were indeed in a stable inn at Bethlehem, he knew what gift they must bring.

"A lamb. We must bring the Savior a gift . . ." he told the others.

"Why a lamb?" someone asked.

"Because the Jews have always brought a lamb . . . a Passover lamb . . . a day of atonement lamb. We have always brought a lamb as a gift to God our Savior."

"Mine," the young shepherd volunteered as he walked over to the flock. Searching through the flock he found his prized lamb—a perfect lamb. "My lamb for the baby Savior."

Mary and the baby were asleep. Joseph dozed on the straw beside them. The journey had been long, the search for lodgings emotionally exhausting. But Joseph's mind was still more active than his body was tired. Joseph heard noises. He bolted upright, fully awake, when he heard the noises coming from outside the stables.

Creeping to the stable door he tried to be silent; he pulled, but the door resisted. The donkey stirred, waking Mary, but the baby Jesus slept on.

"Who is there?" Joseph spoke into the dark courtyard. In the darkness he saw a dozen faces, not the faces of thieves coming to steal from him, but expectant faces.

"We are shepherds," the humble voice of the lead shepherd replied. "Was there a baby born here tonight?"

"Yes."

"We must see Him. We have been told the child is from God." The other shepherds nodded their agreement. They all heard the angels; they all saw the light.

The shepherds had brought a lamp, and they now set the wick of the lantern to give more light. The light was held high, and Joseph saw the yard was filled with shepherds. He opened the obstinate stable door wider.

"Mary," he whispered, so he wouldn't awaken the baby. "Some shepherds want to see Jesus."

Mary stepped to the door, the light revealing the soft features of her face to Joseph. *She was more lovely than ever before,* he thought. His own mother had taught him that a woman's satisfaction makes her more beautiful than she is, and giving birth is among the greatest accomplishments in life. But to Mary, he knew, this birth meant much more. She had obeyed God, and her son would be called the Son of the Highest. Mary was at peace with her dreams.

At Joseph's behest, the shepherds crowded through the stable door, their faces alive with anticipation. But when the light shone upon the baby, the shepherds quickly dropped to their knees with their faces to the ground. They prostrated themselves on the strewn hay in silent adoration.

Several minutes passed as the shepherds worshipped motionless on the ground. Mary and Joseph were transfixed by the sight. Then one of the shepherds lifted his head and repeated the song of the angels:

> *Glory to God in the Highest,*
> *And on earth peace, goodwill toward men.*

As one by one the shepherds looked up at the baby, Mary saw their eyes—crying eyes framed by scruffy beards. Their faces, blackened by the soot of campfires layered upon the dust of the open fields, were now streaked with tears. Mary thought, *These are adoring eyes.*

"I don't understand . . .," Joseph broke the silence.

The lead shepherd told them how they had been keeping watch over their flocks by night, how a host of dazzlingly bright angels had appeared to them in the fields. He told how the shepherds had looked into the light of heaven itself and heard the singing of angels.

The older shepherd stepped forward to gaze at the little one in the manger. "The angel called him our Savior." The shepherd found he no longer doubted God or his salvation. He adored the baby, and Mary saw belief in his eyes.

The younger shepherd whose secret sin had brought him to this place arose, the small, spotless lamb in his arms. He approached the feed trough where Jesus lay sleeping. Placing the lamb in the straw, he said simply,

"For you. This lamb is in my place."

5

AN INTERRUPTING CRISIS AT THE CHANTRY

Melchior Has A Solution

"KNOCK . . . KNOCK . . . KNOCK!"

Magi do not arise early in the morning because they are up at night stargazing. As a matter of fact, magi usually do not awaken and get ready for the day until the middle of the morning, sometimes afternoon.

"KNOCK . . . KNOCK . . . KNOCK!"

The soft steps of Jewel's slippers could be heard on the stone floor. He was hurrying to answer the door before the magi were awakened.

"I am coming . . . ."

Throwing the door open wide, Jewel saw two soldiers standing there, but not just soldiers—soldiers with battle weaponry in hand. Behind them was their leader, the short, stocky Commander who had sliced the leather throngs on Balthazar's wrist. He's the one who whispered to Melchior, "My family were magi." He spoke apologetically, but boldly, "We've come to collect taxes . . . Here everyone must pay taxes including the chantry."

"But magi have never paid taxes . . .," Jewel protested to the soldiers. "Magi have been exempted for ten generations since Gaumata was king." Commander knew that Melchior was from that line. But he had a job to do, and his military rank was more dear to him than blood. He spit out the words,

"This year everyone pays taxes . . . ."

"But my master, Melchior, is a direct descendant of the Gaumata family."

"I have my orders . . . . Everyone this year pays taxes."

"What if we don't pay?" Jewel and the soldiers heard a raspy voice behind them. It was Melchior, fully dressed and prepared for the day. He had been awakened by the loud pounding on the door, gotten dressed quickly, and in a soothing voice that poured oil on troubled waters, "Tell me . . . what will happen if we don't pay your taxes?"

The unshaved face of Commander was grim; he feared the evil power of the magi. He personally knew about sorcery and witchcraft. He did not want to incur the anger of Melchior or any of his fellow magi. Commander wanted to diffuse the situation. He carefully explained, "Soldiers will come and take the front door off your house, then the king will sell it to the highest bidder."

"We don't want that," Melchior said to the gathering crowd. Balthazar and Gasper had joined the confrontation at the front door of the chantry.

"I will go with you to see your governor . . . now!" Melchior pointed to the guards to lead the way. "I will go with you immediately to solve this problem."

Commander explained, "The King of Persia had met unexpected bills, and decided to collect taxes from the chantry of every magi living in the kingdom. As each magi family got larger, some of their sons duplicated their fathers' trades. All across Persia there are new chantries being built. According to the king, they were growing faster than government houses."

Commander's office was a large, square, mud building, with only a few long slits for windows across the top, shaded by the overhanging roof. Out back were several sheds where soldiers slept, ate, and spent their unoccupied hours. Melchior marched into the building like a king to sit behind Commander's table.

His stomach was growling because he had not eaten. But this was important business. Some flies buzzed around the stifling hot room. Commander jumped to get Melchior a chair. He had not expected a magian to visit his sordid office. Otherwise, he would have cleaned out the trash and swept the floor.

"I am honored that you have come to see me . . ." Commander stood in front of his own table to speak to the seated Melchior. "I expected all magi would rebel against the order. I expected you to go straight to the governor, or even the king. I expected that the magi would be stirring up the masses to protest these taxes." Melchior said nothing, just smiled at the expected response.

Commander asked, "But why have you come here to my office?"

"For privacy . . . ."

Commander immediately ordered his solders to leave. He then shut the door.

"Sit down," the elder Melchior instructed. Then he explained, "This issue is greater than taxes and money. The issue is loyalty to our king."

Melchior waited for his answer to sink in before continuing, "Just as soldiers are loyal to their king and obey his commands, so we magi are the king's servants."

Melchior was careful with his words. He wanted his message to go to the governor, even perhaps the king. So he wanted to make sure Commander understood every word he said. But not only the words, but the attitude of his heart.

Melchior explained, "Soldiers serve the king with their brute strength. They defend Persia from all attacks. When necessary, they launch war against all enemies of Persia. Soldiers are rewarded when they have won a victory. What greater honor for the soldier when the king read his name in front of all the troops and then gives him a reward of a house, or slaves, or cattle."

Commander was no longer defensive. Melchior was

making a friend. And this friend would deliver the message correctly to the governor and the king.

Melchior continued his proclamation. "Magi serve the king with wisdom from the stars; magi tell how to make decisions and when to make right decisions. When the king is blessed, all his people are blessed. Magi also serve the king with magic. You know that Zoroaster did away with the hundreds of gods that were once worshiped in Persia, and he simplified it into two forces: Ahura and Mazda. Magi have wisdom that's given to those who seek Ahura, the good force of the universe. The other opposing force is Angra Mainyu, which is the destructive spirit. It's the evil spirit. It's the force magi use to direct negative spirits to bring harm and destruction on their enemies.

"Yes, sir . . . Yes, sir."

"Tell our governor that magi will pay their fair share of taxes, just as much as the members of the governor's court pay, and just as much as the members of the king's court pay. We do not object to giving our king money; we give to him our wisdom which brings blessings to the king, governor, and you, Commander. But if the governor and king do not treat all fairly, he can expect the destructive spirit of Angra Mainyu through his angry subjects."

Melchior walked out of Commander's office, turned left and headed towards the chantry and home. Slowly . . . dignified steps without fear. He dared not look back for that would show doubt and fear. But in his heart he knew what would happen. Then he heard the horse being mounted. Commander's boots prodded the white stallion into a gallop, and then the horse broke into a run. Melchior knew that his message would be delivered to the governor.

Later Melchior stood in the tall receiving room of the governor's palace. He looked up at the golden ceiling and gleaming walls and the flawless marble floors which were swept constantly. Sandals tracking sand across marble left streaks, but the sand was almost instantly swept by servants. Melchior expected to be called into the governor's official receiving room, but no. He was ushered into the private chambers to meet the governor informally.

He was a chubby, balding man with wrinkled eyes and a pudgy nose pushed up like the snout of a pig. The governor commented on the message send him by Commander.

He was appreciative that Melchior had not ranted and made threats to the soldiers or any of their leaders. Rather than protesting and refusing to pay their taxes, Melchior had offered a solution, and the governor was glad to hear of it further.

"How shall he tax each of the chantries?" the governor began the conversation.

Melchior wanted to point out that the governor could avoid taxing the magi and yet that was not the first thing he wanted to discuss. He suggested to the governor, "If you tax the chantries, the magi will incite the people, and the mobs will protest in front of the palace. You don't want that!"

"Oh no . . ., no . . ., no . . . ."

"Then I suggest that we not tax each of the chantries, but rather allow each magian an opportunity to give respect to the king by making a financial donation to the king's treasury.

Melchior explained, "The greatest contribution to the governor and king would be the wisdom that each magian would share. Along with their wisdom, allow each magian to contribute to the king's treasury–money equal to the size of the chantry–money in the form of gold or silver coins."

Melchior paused to suggest the magi receive money from the people to give them good blessings of Ahura Mazda, or that some magi receive money when they threaten people with a curse from Angra Mainyu.

Then Melchior explained, "Both your governor and the king have members of your court who assist you; in return, they don't pay taxes on their homes. We magi consider ourselves as important as your advisors. But your advisors can give you money in many other ways, just as we magi."

Then Melchior moved toward his conclusion, "Treat your magi and your advisors the same."

The chubby governor nodded approval.

Melchior then carefully outlined a plan where the magi and advisors in the king's court would make a donation to the king's treasury equal to the size of the home that each owned.

Melchior said the magi would agree, the court advisors would agree, but none wanted to pay taxes. "So let's call it a donation to the king's treasury."

"Agreed . . .," the eyes of the fat governor squinted with glee. "We will call it a donation."

As Melchior rose to leave, he returned to his original purpose for coming to see the governor. "The king wants more money from the magi. If a donation is also received from the court advisors, he'll get twice as much as he planned."

Melchior smiled, "Think about it . . . twice as much money."

6

WHAT DO WE KNOW ABOUT THE COMING KING?

....

The Star is about Him

After Melchior returned from seeing the governor, he found the other two magi asleep. Usually the magi took a nap during the hottest part of the day—1:00 to 3:00 pm. Sometimes they slept in their private chamber on a stone bed extended from the wall. Today, they had taken a nap on the patio at the rear of the chantry.

After their nap, magi usually ate their midday meal under the shade of the eucalyptus tree. While this afternoon meal was not heavy, magi considered eating a religious ceremony. Just as the Assyrians sacrificed their food to their "gods," the magi sect considered eating food an oblation; they considered eating an act of worship to their god(s), whoever he or she may be, an exercise in religious intimacy with God.

Balthazar did not acquire the religious eating ritual of the Persian magi. The Ethiopian ate for enjoyment, and he enjoyed it in silence—that meant he didn't talk while eating. But his meal couldn't be called silent. Just as Melchior ate sacrificially according to his magi cult, and Gaspar ate, respectively, like those trained to be a European king, so Balthazar chewed loudly according to Ethiopian customs. Noisy chewing was his way of showing appreciation. Each ate according to his own culture, yet each respected the divinity of the other—each tolerated the other.

Melchior didn't talk while eating because the Persian magi communed with God as they ate, so the other two magi ate in silence. Their silence was in deference to their friend.

While Balthazar didn't talk, he did make noises. His smacks showed enjoyment. Sounds came from his mouth . . . slurping . . . chewing . . . and an occasional belch.

"Um-m-m-m," the Ethiopian said constantly.

No one spoke as each slowly consumed the food. Even though the quantity of food was sparse, the main meal took as long to eat as a banquet—no one hurrying, no one talking, no one making eye contact.

Jewel sat in the shade at the other end of the patio. He waited until everyone finished eating before stirring. He sat motionless because on previous occasions he had been reprimanded for movement that broke the magis' contemplation. Even when the magi took a last bite, Jewel didn't move.

I will count to one hundred before I move, Jewel thought to himself. The patio was as silent as the noon sun, as still as nature tolerating the sun overhead.

"Crack," then "pop," the stones in the wall of the house talked as they expanded under the torrid sun.

"B-z-z-z-z-z-z-z- . . .," an insect broke the comfortable silence.

Ninety-seven ... ninety-eight ... ninety-nine ... one hundred, Jewel moved one leg to rise, then waited. Then he moved the second leg and waited again.

Nothing . . ., no response from his three masters. He slowly arose and, walking without any noise, as though his feet didn't touch the floor, he bent over the outdoor fireplace to blow carefully on the black ashes until he coaxed one small red ember. Again, he blew carefully—too much wind or he'd blow the red embers out—too little breath, no small dancing flame.

Within a few minutes a solitary flame was heating the pot of water. Because water will never boil if watched, Jewel busied himself chopping the thin dark tea leaves into narrow strips.

Jewel thought, *The tea must have life to give life; it gives robust life in the tea cup. When the tea leaf suffers death in the boiling water, it gives its life to those who drink it.* Again he entertained those thoughts that came only from his past. *We enjoy its abundance because the tea leaf gives its life for us.*

Jewel knew that was God's plan for life. Always–life springs from death. A kernel of wheat had to fall into the ground to die, then life springs forth in a new stalk of wheat. But not just one new kernel of wheat, but an abundance of new kernels live because one died.

As Jewel lifted the tray of cups, he intentionally scraped his feet on the sandy stones. He warned the three magi that he was coming. Also, he wanted to challenge their palates, he silently thought. It was his way of breaking the seclusion of silence.

Tea must be anticipated to be enjoyed.

Then setting down the tray, he purposefully touched two cups together so a tiny sound captured everyone's attention.

"Ting . . ."

When the servant realized he had their attention and knew they were ready for their concentration to be broken, Jewel was the first to speak,

"Tea . . . Jewel tea."

The three savored their drink. Melchior smiled, then asked, "I wonder if we'll have tea in heaven?"

"Ha . . .," the beautiful bass voice of Balthazar rang out. Loudly, he began to quote what he learned as a boy.

> *"Since God will prepare a table before me*
> *In the presence of our enemies,*
> *He will probably serve tea.*
> *The Lord will anoint my head with the oil of prosperity,*

My tea cup runs over.
Surely goodness and mercy shall chase after me
All the days of my life
And I will live in the house of the Lord
Forever"
(Psalm 23)

"Where did that come from?" Gasper, the inquisitive one, asked.

"From the Psalms," Balthazar answered, "the twenty-third one."

Then the Ethiopian told how the queen of his country—called Sheba—went to visit the king in Jerusalem. She had heard about the wealth and splendor of King Solomon. Even Solomon's servants wore clothes of royalty. She had heard that silver was as plenteous as the stones on the streets of Jerusalem.

"You know women are curious," Balthazar laughed.

He continued, "The Ethiopian queen was as beautiful as Solomon was wise, but even the wisest of men is dumb in the presence of the most beautiful woman in the world."

All laughed nervously.

"King Solomon wanted to have sex with her, but she refused until she got what she wanted." Then with a twinkle in his eye Balthazar remarked, "You know, sex first entices a man, then second makes him obedient. Then a woman uses her sex to make the man her slave."

Again, they laughed.

"King Solomon possessed a book that was the secret of the Jews' strength; it was their scroll of worship and praise to God. The book contained songs that men sung to God to show their love and worship of Him. In response to worship, the God of heaven blessed the Jews. The book is called Psalms.

"King Solomon's father, David, had written most of the Psalms on this scroll. Because of the blessing of their Jehovah

God, David had become the most powerful king in his region of the world. David's heart was strong because of God. David's kingdom was strong because of worship. A man doesn't have it within himself to be strong—there's too much evil—a man gets his strength from outside himself. David got his strength from God.

The Queen of Sheba wanted to bring the book of Psalms back to Ethiopia. Solomon wouldn't give her David's scroll, but he had it copied for her. However, the Queen wouldn't give him sex until she got her copy of the scroll. You know it's said,

"Sex attracts a man; he can't wait to satisfy himself. He yearns to take sex before it's time. A woman has time on her side; she waits until she possesses what she desires, then she gives the man what he wants."

The three kings laughed at the proverb, for they recognized truth in those words. Then Balthazar explained, "When the Queen of Sheba returned to Ethiopia, she had a copy of Psalms in her hand. She decreed that a copy be made for all the sons of the palace. She wanted the sons of her palace to be strong because they would read the Psalms of David . . . and memorize them . . . and meditate on them . . . and live by them."

"I can quote much of it from memory," Balthazar answered. "I will quote one of my favorite passages. It's about the coming King who will rule the Jews. This King is the Lord."

> *"The Lord said to the other LORD,*
> *Sit at my right hand where the next King sits,*
> *I will make your enemies your footstool'"*
> (Psalm 110:1).

The other two magi, Melchior and Gaspar, thought about the dilemma of two LORDS in heaven. Then Melchior spoke—because the older usually spoke first. "Is that David the warrior speaking of his son Solomon offering him a seat by his side until their enemies are destroyed?"

Gasper waited till Melchior had completely finished with nothing else to add. Then Gaspar, the youngest magi, commented,

"I don't think it's David speaking to Solomon," Gasper again waited to hear any negative answers, then added, "the Lord is not a human king speaking to his human son, but it seems to be God speaking to God. That means God has a Son, and God will make His Son a King."

Then Balthazar added the next verse from the Psalm:

The LORD shall
Send the sword of His son's strength out of Zion,
The Son shall rule over His enemies!
The Lord's people shall submit to the Son's power,
They shall submit to the beauty of His holiness.
The Son shall come from the womb of the morning
He shall have the freshness of youth (Psalm 110:2-3).

Again it was the duty of ancient wisdom to speak, so Melchior spoke the obvious, "The Lord in heaven gives His Son rule over his enemies."

"Also," Melchior added, "the Lord's people gladly follow their King."

"BUT," Balthazar raised an objection, "But, how does the LORD in heaven come down to earth?" Then answering his question with a question, the Ethiopian asked,

"Does the Lord—the King—come to earth on a lightning bolt in a storm? Does he come in a comet? Does He come to Mount Olympus to the Parthenon in Athens, Greece?"

"No!" the older Melchior answered. "He comes from the womb of the morning." But no one knew what that meant.

Then the aged questioner asked again, "And who is the

mother called 'morning' who gives birth to the Son who will be King? And how will heaven's King come to earth?" Melchior asked.

The room was silent. Melchior and Balthazar didn't know the answer, just as one of the Assyrian magicians (magi who use incantations) didn't know. And just as the wise philosophers of Greece didn't know.

"I know," Gaspar answered the apparently unanswerable question.

Both men looked surprised at their younger friend. Gaspar reminded them of the scroll he had hidden in his tunic–the one written by Isaiah, the Hebrew prophet.

"Isaiah says much about the coming king." Gaspar explained the Jewish Deliverer would come as a child; he would be a son, not a daughter. "The ruler would not be a queen like the Greeks worship Athena, who ruled in wisdom from the Acropolis in Athens where the Parthenon was built."

Gaspar quoted Isaiah, "'*For unto us a Child is born, unto us a Son is given; and the government will be upon His shoulder.*' (Isa. 9:6). The child will be born like other children, except He'll be the Son of God."

Gaspar explained that he had read the passage many times, and that he had thought about each word in the passage many times. He explained, "If the King will be born as a child, I should like to see that child."

Gaspar continued, "The King would come from heaven, so God sends this Son who lives in heaven to earth as a little baby."

Melchior asked the obvious question: "But how shall the LORD who is the King of heaven enter the womb of a woman to be born on earth?"

Gaspar answered, "The Isaiah scroll also tells us the baby will be born as a sign or a miracle.

'Behold, I send you a sign, a virgin shall conceive and bear a Son, and shall call His name Immanuel (God with us)'"
(Isa. 7:14).

"That means God will come to us by a virgin," Melchior said.

"That means the child will be born through a miracle," Balthazar added.

"We must look for a virgin to find our King," Gaspar explained. "When we find our child born to a virgin, we will find the King of the Jews." The youngest magi continued,

'"He shall not judge after the sight of the eyes, nor after the hearing of the ears, but He shall judge by righteousness. He will smite the earth with the authority of His words, and the judgment of His mouth, and He will destroy all the wicked'"
(Isa. 11:4).

"Every king has made mistakes," Melchior added. "Does this mean this Jewish King shall never be wrong?"

Gaspar again took control of the conversation, "Listen to what the earth will be like after the King-Judge is finished with His judgment.

'The wolf shall lie peacefully with the lamb, and the leopard shall lie down with the small goat. The calf and the lion will feed together, and a little child shall lead them. The cow and the bear shall feed together, and their young will sleep together in peace. The lion will become a vegetarian, for it will eat straw. And a baby will play with a cobra, and not get hurt'"
(Isa. 11:6-8).

Melchior and Balthazar had never heard anything like that before. Then the wise Melchior said,

"The Jewish Child-Deliverer will have power to change everything on earth. The predator will no longer attack us. All evil men will be destroyed, and no will murder."

"We are closer to our answer than we ever thought," the wise Melchior announced. Both magi looked at the older Persian sage for an answer. What did he mean, "*We are closer to our answer?*"

"The specular star we saw last night—and the other magi didn't see it—is God's sign to us."

Melchior explained that just as Balthazar had access to the Jewish holy book, the Psalms, and Gaspar had access to another Jewish holy book, Isaiah, so he had access to the books of Moses.

Melchior explained how Daniel, a Jewish prophet, was taken captive to Babylon. This Daniel was a magi to the kings of Babylon, and his wisdom helped guide that nation. Then Melchior's people, the Persians, defeated Babylon and brought Daniel to the capital of Persia to be a counselor to the King of Persia.

"Daniel brought his holy books, the writings of Moses, to Persia. We magi have studied Moses to learn the secret of God's blessings on the Jews," Melchior explained.

"We saw a spectacular star last evening. Listen to what God said about stars when He created everything.

> *"Let bright lights appear in the sky*
> *To separate night from the day.*
> *Let there be two great lights,*
> *The sun to rule the day, and the moon the night.*
> *Let stars appear with their illuminous light,*
> *These lights will be for signs to men.*
> *These stars will mark off season, the days and years.*
> *They will count time for mankind"*
> (Genesis 1:14-18).

Melchior explained that the magi studied the stars to understand the meaning of life and its purpose. He elaborated that God called Abraham as the Father of the Jewish nation. God brought Abraham out in the night,

> *"Look up into the heavens to see the stars,*
> *You will be Father of a nation like them.*
> *Count the stars if you can,*
> *Your people will be like the stars.*
> *So many you can't count them"*
> (Genesis 15:5-6).

Melchior explained that God was interested in the stars, and He created a vast multitude of them because He liked stars. But more than that, God explained time to us by the stars.

"And God spoke to us last night by a star—a spectacular star."

When Melchior mentioned the star they saw the previous evening, he had their full attention. God promised He would reveal His Deliverer would be announced by a star.

> *"I see the Deliverer coming in the future,*
> *I perceive He is coming but not now.*
> *A star will come from the family of Jacob,*
> *He will receive the scepter to rule Israel.*
> *He will crush the enemies of God's people,*
> *He will take captive the people of the world.*
> *He will rule over all the lands,*
> *He will lead Israel valiantly"*
> (Numbers 24:17-18).

"Gentlemen . . .," Melchior announced, "the star we saw last night was announcing the coming of the Jewish King."

"Perhaps the Child-Deliverer was born last night," Gaspar added from his insight, "born to a virgin."

"Perhaps I shall save this discussion for another day," Melchior concluded, rising to his feet. "Perhaps I shall understand it better after I have slept in my quarters." As he left the rooftop, he nodded to Jewel,

"The tea was invigorating; where did you find it?"

"I grew it myself in the shade of the well."

"What remarkable insight," Gaspar innocently commented, "no one does that around here. Where did you get that idea?"

Jewel weighed his words, then answered, "The world's best tea is grown in dark, damp areas, where the ground is eternally wet like a swamp."

"Swamp?" Melchior quizzed over the word. "What's a swamp? I know many words, but I've never heard the word *swamp*."

"There are places where water lies at the roots of trees, and vines grow too thick to walk. Trees are taller and thicker than the cedars of the Lebanese Mountains. They are so high the rays from the noonday sun never reach the ground. It is there the best tea in the world is grown."

"There's no place like that; I can't believe it if I haven't seen it."

Jewel smiled as though he wanted to say something, but all he said was, "You can believe the fire is hot when it burns you, and you can believe water is wet when you touch it; so there must be such places when you taste tea that is more unusual than you've ever tasted."

"Have you seen it?"

All Jewel said was, "I've been around."

7

DON'T LOSE YOUR HEAD OVER TAXES

....

Be Mindful of Disobedience

"*Knock . . . knock . . . knock . . . .*" Again it was early morning, and all were asleep in the chantry. It had been two days since the soldiers demanded taxes. Melchior had gone to the governor to arrange a deal so the magi could make a donation to the king's treasury. They didn't have to pay taxes. As far as Melchior was concerned, that package was wrapped up, not to be opened. He wanted to turn his full attention to studying the spectacular star. The elderly magi had proof in the Circle Room that demonstrated the star was not an ordinary star. He could prove it was supernatural if he had time to get into the Circle Room. *Should I take Balthazar and Gaspar into the Circle Room?*

"KNOCK . . . KNOCK . . . KNOCK . . ."

Jewel was first to the door, squinting through the bright sunrise to see Commander and soldiers standing there again. But this time they were no armaments.

"We've come to measure the house," Commander's stern voice echoed into the house, loud enough to awaken the three magi.

"Go ahead and measure the house." Jewel stepped outside, closing the door behind him. He pointed to the left and right, waving his arms, "Measure north and south, east and west."

"No, I've been instructed to measure inside and outside,"

Commander barked. "I must come in to measure the Circle Room." Commander pushed his way through the unlocked door. Jewel protested, but Commander insisted, "I must measure both inside and out."

"THAT IS IMPOSSIBLE," Melchior's loud, stern voice rolled down the hallway. "No one is allowed in the Circle Room. All my archaeological studies are there." Then to emphasize the point, "I have not allowed Jewel or the other magi into my room; no one is allowed in that room. You cannot measure it."

"I have my orders."

"No, I told you. You cannot come in."

Then Melchior suggested to the Commander, "I will go with you to see the governor. There must be some mistake. Perhaps your orders were not communicated properly." Melchior explained that when he talked with the governor they decided to measure all the houses outside. "Let us go together to see the governor. Jewel will get my camel; you may rid your stallion. We will talk to him together."

Melchior mounted his camel and followed Commander to the Hall of the Governor. But his thoughts were not on the Circle Room. He couldn't get his mind off the spectacular star he and the others saw a few months ago. Melchior thought, *Why do these interruptions keep me from thinking about the compelling star I saw in the western sky? I should be studying my charts in the Circle Room instead of tending to these little business interruptions.*

Melchior was gone most of the morning while Jewel and Gaspar busied themselves around the chantry. It was then that Balthazar asked Jewel, "Have you never been in the Circle Room?"

"No."

"Why have you never been in the Circle Room?"

"Melchior keeps his studies and research secret; I don't know what he is doing."

Balthazar thought about the situation and decided to wait, "I will ask Melchior to show me the room when he returns."

"Me, too," agreed Gaspar.

Balthazar thought to himself, *What is so secret in that room so that Melchior will not tell the world? If he has found some great truth, magi pride would motivate him to tell everyone.*

"Look!" Melchior yelled into the chantry as he returned from the Governor's palace. "We don't have to allow soldiers into our chantry." He came back from the governor holding a scroll in his hand exempting his chantry. Because Melchior's house was circular, it could not be measured on the outside north to south and east to west. However, all the other chantries were square so they had to be measured inside and out. Since Melchior's chantry was the only round one, it had the only exception.

Melchior spent the next few days going from chantry to chantry, telling the different magi of the plan to make a donation to the king's treasury. He was visiting the same chantry where he had gone a few days before to ask about the spectacular star in the west. Melchior remembered some magi had almost laughed at him when he mentioned a star arising in the west. Melchior decided he would not mention the supernatural star on this visit. He wanted to get the support of all the magi, not use this trip to tell them about the spectacular star he had seen. Melchior told the different magi, "Our money will not be called taxes; it's our donation to our nation, Persia, in appreciation for living in peace and freedom."

Most of the magi accepted the explanation of Melchior and agreed to make their donation. They especially liked the explanation to not call it taxes.

"I told the governor and king that we would make a donation in money, just as we make a donation in wisdom." Melchior told the Governor that magi wisdom not only guided the king in making decisions, but more importantly, the magi wisdom helped keep the population from rebelling—or as he put it, "Keep them peacefully committed to the king." In essence, the king was using the magi to keep the peace and spread his official propaganda. All seemed to agree.

But Saduj, a hotheaded magi, rudely received Melchior and argued with him. "Melchior, I know why you've come. You want me to pay taxes." Saduj hated taxes and kept telling Melchior, "Taxes called by any other name are still taxes; I will not pay them."

Melchior reasoned with him; first using peer pressure. "Because all other magi are marking a donation, why would Saduj not join them to make a donation?

"Taxes by any other name are still taxes."

Then Melchior appealed to Saduj's prestigious position among the magi. "Since you have great wisdom, share with the king your understanding so all magi may have the king as a friend, not an enemy."

"Taxes by any other name are still taxes."

Then Melchior appealed to Saduj's influence. "All people respect you as a magi and will listen to you; let's use your position for peace to keep the people from rebellion."

"Taxes by any other name are still taxes."

Two weeks later, Saduj was called into an audience with the king. Soldiers put him in shackles and rode him in a cart to the king's court. As the soldiers were leaving, they tore the front door off Saduj's chantry. That told everyone the king now owned Saduj's house and could sell it for taxes.

"No . . .," Saduj yelled profanities at the soldiers as the cart drove off. The cart was the king's way of humiliating him; no horse for his dignity, no camel for his acceptance.

Saduj had intended to wear his magi vesture, the power symbols of the magi office, when he saw the king. But no, with shackles . . . and clothes of the common man . . . and stripped of all symbols of power . . . Saduj stood isolated before the king.

The king had a difficult decision. He didn't want to offend all the magi, and he certainly didn't want the magi to create a revolt among the people. Yet, Saduj was defiant and apparently would not listen to reason. Would he use Saduj as an example? It was a risky decision.

"What shall I do with you?" the king spoke to Saduj, trying to appeal to his human instinct. "I've tried to be nice to all magi, but you defy me. I respect all magi, and I fear their wrath. But you are guilty of defying my orders." The king turned to his court and said,

"What do you say in this matter?"

A trusted advisor stepped forward to announce, "I have a word from Melchior that he and all the magi respect and revere you, King." The king nodded in approval. The advisor continued, "Melchior advises the king that he and all other magi repudiate Saduj and do not stand with him." The advisor went on to say that Melchior promised that all the magi would support the king and promote peace among the people, even defying what Saduj the magi might say or do.

He looked at his advisor for assurance, "Is this the true word of Melchior?"

"Yes."

"Let it be known to my advisor that if his words are not true, he'll pay a price."

"They are true."

The king turned to Saduj and said, "You have heard what has been said by other magi. How do you answer your king?"

Saduj lifted up his shackled hands to his chest to loudly shout, "I speak the truth, and Melchior is a traitor to all magi." Saduj continued to berate, "Melchior and all other magi are blinded by the evil forces of **Agra Mainya**." Then in a final act of defiance, he spit out his challenge to the king.

"I am a true magi and loyal to Zoroastrianism, which is our belief. The magi have never paid taxes; if I pay taxes, I have denied my calling and my commitment to the gods."

But the king argued back,

"But you are not paying taxes; you are making a donation. You will be like all other members of this court who support your government."

"Taxes by any other name are taxes."

"I will not argue with you over the meaning of word," the king said to Saduj. "My decree is that you must make the donation or else."

Saduj stood for a moment. He slowly turned full circle to see everyone in the room. He glared into the face of each advisor, each member of the court, and each guard. Finally, he glared at the king, looking definitely into his eyes.

"By the power of *Agra Mainyu*, I denounce you, O king. You're not fit to sit upon this throne." Then Saduj turned to the advisors, pointing an angry finger and hurling the same angry insult, "I denounce you, Advisors, by the power of *Angra Mainyu*." The advisors stiffened. Some were afraid of the curses that were cast by other magi. At the same time, some sneered and laughed. They did not believe in evil curses.

Saduj turned to the guards to curse them, "By the power of *Angra Mainyu*, I curse all of you." Soldiers, fearless in battle, before the onslaught of a vehement, religious condemnation.

Then Saduj turned to the king and proclaimed,

"By the power of *Angra Mainyu*, I condemn your soul to hell; may you rot in the flames of eternal punishment."

"Enough!!!" the king shouted to his soldiers, "Gag him. Don't let him speak again. *Gag* him."

The group of soldiers rushed Saduj, quickly stuffing a rag in his mouth. Wrestling the struggling Saduj to the ground, the warriors gagged him as tightly as possible. Yet, he still spewed hatred with his eyes,

"Ugh . . . ugh . . . ugh . . . "

"Take him to the courtyard and behead him . . . ***NOW***! Bring his head back to me in five minutes . . .," the king barked his orders as the men dragged the struggling Saduj out of the courtroom.

The king sat on his throne fuming, but saying nothing. The court members began whispering among themselves, and the king angrily glared at them. Suddenly, the room fell silent. No one moved.

And then from the courtyard could be heard the scraping of chains across a rock floor. Then everyone heard one mighty word, "**STRIKE.**"

"**SWISSSSSSH.**" The scimitar, the curved sword of the Near East, first cut through the air, then through Saduj's neck. The sound of chains rumpling to the floor could be heard by all in the courtroom.

Then, "**THUD.**"

Next, they heard the sound of marching feet triumphantly entering the king's courtroom. They brought their trophy mounted on a spear—the head of Saduj.

"Post it by the main gate for all to see," the angry king barked to his soldiers. Then he turned abruptly to his scribe to write the following and post it on the outer door,

"Saduj defied the king and all the magi of Persia."

8

A CONTINUING DISCUSSION ABOUT THE STAR

....

Jewel's Parable

The biting wind and the grey, muddy sky made the day seem much colder than usual, chilling the hands, feet, and mind. Melchior wrapped in his heaviest coat, then covered himself with a blanket. But his eyes were not closed in sleep. His active mind was pondering,

No one had ever documented an aurora like the brightness we saw in the Western sky. Why were we given the privilege to see the spectacular star?

Melchior's thoughts perplexed him,

Should they act on a star that they only saw once?" He kept badgering himself with another question, *"Was the star really there, or was I only imagining a star in my mind. I didn't see the star until Jewel pointed it out. Did he plant an idea in my mind that wasn't there?*

The thin-skinned Ethiopian hated the cold and was huddled close to the charcoal fire in the kitchen. Jewel thought Balthazar might eventually burn himself, but he didn't disturb him. Jewel knew Balthazar was in deep thought, so he didn't interrupt his thinking.

How could I see a light that no one else saw? Balthazar knew he saw the addictive light; he could not look away—he couldn't close his mind. He couldn't get the spectacular star out of his thoughts. It was the brightest star he had ever seen; he would not deny his eyes. He had never experienced such a spectacle in his whole life.

Balthazar struggled in his thoughts, *Lord, why did You show me the light? Yet the magi in the other chantry didn't see it.* Then he corrected himself, *No other magi but Melchior and Gaspar?*

Balthazar felt God was trying to tell him something, so he prayed over and over, *"Lord, tell me more!"*

Gaspar hadn't joined the others for the first meal of the day. He was still hunkered down in his bed where he slept. He was not wrapped in his blanket trying to sleep. He was face down, praying, his knees drawn up under his body, his arms outstretched. Gaspar couldn't get the star out of his mind,

"Lord, I know You let us see the star for a purpose," but the purpose escaped him.

"Lord, show us the star again," the light-skinned magi pleaded sincerely with God. *"Show me the star again so I'll know what to do."*

"Please . . . please . . . please . . . ."

Sometimes God shuts heaven up for a reason. Sometimes God does not speak a second time because He said all we needed to hear the first time. Then Gaspar added, "At least God doesn't show us something a second time, because we saw all we needed to see."

So God didn't talk with Gaspar that morning. God didn't have anything else to tell him. It was as though God was waiting for the three magi to act on what they saw. And isn't that faith? Acting on what God shows you?

But the doubter wants God to say it again, and again, and again. They want God to show them more and more and more. They want God to bring something else into their life to prod them into action.

The magi were controlled by their doubts. Doesn't

doubt happen when you know what to do, but something inside says "wait" or "I need more information" or "I want to be sure before I take a leap of faith?" If God was going to do something else to move the kings to action, perhaps that something else was Jewel.

Jewel busied himself, then went to the dark, wet spot in the garden well where the tea leaves grew. Picking the choicest dark leaves, he returned to the preparation board. There he carefully chopped the leaves into long, narrow strips, saying to himself, *"The leaves must die to give us its nourishment."* Jewel knew that death was the rule of heaven. It was also the rule of nature to give its riches when it dies.

The kettle sang its happy song as steam drifted out its spout. Jewel carefully poured the dancing water into each cup, the thin-lipped ceramic cup for Melchior, the earthen mug for Balthazar, and the carved stone cup for Gasper. Jewel breathed a prayer that the tea would open the hearts of his three masters for what he planned to tell them. He knew what would assemble them to the dining table.

"Ting . . . ting . . . ting . . . ."

Jewel gently rapped a spoon on the thin tea cup. Its tiny ring carried throughout the whole chantry. The tiny ring could not be ignored, interrupting the thoughts of all three magi. There's something about the thought of an enjoyable drink that can't easily be brushed aside. Then they heard the invitation:

"Tea time!"

As they entered the dining area to huddle around the warm fire, Jewel announced, "Make yourself comfortable by the fire; I have a parable to tell you."

"Once there was a man who knew all about tea, and he brewed the best tea in the world. Because he loved the aroma of tea, he learned that tea must be grown away from the sun, away from its penetrating, hot rays, in a damp, shadowy place. So he gave his life to grow the most exquisite tea leaves ever. However, once the leaves are grown, it's not beautiful tea to behold, nor is it soft tea to touch; it is only life-satisfying in the taste. But for the tea to accomplish the purpose for which God put it upon this earth, it must give its life for one moment in time—it must give its life for the tea drinker.

"Time is short; time exists in the eye of the human beholder. What may be considered two minutes for a tea leaf may be compared to seven years for magi. But for God, time is eternal. And this tea is given for your enjoyment; the tea has given its life for you. Just as God put each tea leaf on this earth for a purpose, God has put you on this earth for a purpose. The tea leaf is not here to serve itself, but others, so you are on this earth for a purpose. God wants to use you for only a few moments of time for a special purpose."

The magi didn't know what the parable meant, but they examined its depth. For the speaker of a parable never gives his intent superficially, but rather hides its meaning in the intricacies of the story.

Each of the hopeful kings sat contemplating their empty tea cups, mulling over the mystery of the parable.

"More tea?" Jewel looked each man deeply in the eye before passing on to the next set of eyes.

"No," Melchior spoke for the others, "no more tea. I would like to hear more of the parable to understand its meaning."

"God has put a great jewel in your hand. The jewel that God has given to you is to see His star in one moment of time. That star tells you to do something for the Kingdom—God's Kingdom—even though you will not be the supreme rulers in His Kingdom.

"God is not looking for the three of you to rule in His Kingdom, but to magnify His Kingdom. Multiply his Kingdom . . . and help the King of Kings rule the earth. The King is born, so you must represent your kingdom and carry gifts to the Baby-King.

The three wise men knew better than to ask a question when they'd only heard half of what Jewel was saying.

"Only God draws a straight line, as Melchior told us the other day. Every straight line extends into infinity, and only God is infinite."

Gaspar wondered where Jewel's logic was going, for Gaspar thought as a rational European, i.e., more rational than the emotional African magian or the wise magian of Persia.

Jewel continued, "We must live in a circle, for we are finite, and all that goes around must return to its beginning. The moon goes around and returns a month later. The sun goes around and returns a year later. And so we live in this circle of time. Now we must take what has been given us, and go . . . Do what kings must do when a baby is born in an adjoining kingdom."

Jewel got up to stoke the fire. He watched the small flame lick the bottom of the tea kettle. The magi understood the action; it was a scholarly thing, "You must watch what I do before I tell you what I mean." Then turning to the three, with kettle in hand, Jewel turned to the three to invite,

"More tea . . . it's Jewel tea."

When Jewel finished pouring more tea, he went and crouched on his haunches as a servant would do, refusing to sit on a chair as equal with his master. But also Jewel refused to sit on the floor as an animal. From his crouched position, Jewel began to explain,

"God in His circumstances has brought three uncrowned kings together on the 25th day of the 12th month. You are the three kings that are the three stars from the band of Sirius, the Eastern star.

"Each of you knows something of the book—God's Word—where God has predicted what is going to happen in the future.

"You, Melchior, have learned of God's prophecy to bless Abraham and his seed, the Jews. You have seen that God compares all of the Jews to stars. You have read of the prophecy of Balaam—from this Eastern region—who said that the Deliverer would be predicted by a star."

Jewel complimented the faith of Melchior that he believed God's promise of a star and was searching the Scriptures to find it.

"We saw the spectacular star on the 25th day of the 12th month; now we face a new day and a new challenge. You must act upon what you have learned about the star from God. You cannot bring yesterday back for a second look. You can only prepare for tomorrow. You must act upon the star God showed you in the Western horizon." The servant was not telling his master what he must do; rather, Jewel told Melchior what God wanted him to do. "Now you must do what God has called you to accomplish in this moment of time."

Then Jewel concluded his remarks to his master, "God has given you great insight about the universe. You understand that we live in a circle of time. You are the Circle Maker. Now you must begin a new circle of time for a baby that is born to rule the universe."

Then Jewel turned to his Ethiopian magi, "You, Balthazar, have brought us the great knowledge of the Psalms. You have told us that the LORD in heaven spoke to another Lord in heaven promising to make Him a King upon the earth. That second King is to be a Priest King Who will bring salvation to all people on earth. You have told us that the King not only will rule, He will be a Priest-King, who will save us. You must act on what you now know in the Psalms about the Messiah King. You must complete the destiny for which God has appointed you.

"Now, Gaspar," Jewel said to the young magian from Europe, "you brought with you the scroll of Isaiah, the prophet. You told us how the Deliverer would come to the earth by a virgin birth. You told us that the government would be upon His shoulders. You told us a Son would be born, and that a Child would be given. The Deliverer would not descend from heaven in an epiphany, but would come through a human birth as all children to this earth. The Deliverer would be Man, and yet the Deliverer would be born as a man. Yet the Deliverer would be God."

"Now here's what the three of you must do." Jewel spoke again with an authoritative voice. "The three of you must go to the Holy Land to find this king."

Melchior spoke first, "How can we find a King somewhere in the West?"

"When you find the star, you'll find the baby," was Jewel's only answer.

Balthazar said, "And what should we do when we find this Baby-King?"

Again Jewel spoke authoritatively, "You will give to this newborn King what any ruling monarch gives to a child born in a nearby kingdom. You will bring Him gifts from your kingly authority to recognize His greatness."

Gaspar asked the next question, "When should we leave on this pilgrimage?"

Again Jewel assumed the role of authority, for none of the kings had questioned his direction to them thus far. The role had reversed; the most brilliant of men were asking questions of their servant. The uncrowned kings ordained by God for a divine purpose were receiving orders from the one who served them.

Gaspar explained, "The journey is over 1,200 miles and you must cross the Tigris River, and then the Euphrates River. You must leave the Eastern world and enter the West. Then you must cross the Barada River near Damascus, and, finally, cross the Jordan River. It is a long, difficult journey, and it may take many months to get there."

"A year is a long time to a child anxious to grow. He looks for things to do because he has time on his hands. But to old men, time goes by very quickly. A year will sweep by as quickly as a western wind."

One year . . ., thought Melchior. *It will take six months to get there, and six months to return. Shall I spend one of my remaining years on this journey?*

Jewel knew his thoughts and had an answer, "What else are you going to do with your time if you don't spend a year to go present your gifts to the Child-King?" Then he added, "What else in life can be greater than worshiping the Child-King, or giving gifts to the Child-King?"

Melchior interrupted, "That could be the reason for which we were born!"

But I've never travelled beyond the Euphrates River; it's a long distance, Melchior thought.

Again Jewel answered almost as though he could read minds, "Your barrier is not the river, nor is it the desert; it is not even the threatening mountains you cross. You'll have to cross the doubts of your own heart. Your greatest barriers are in your mind. You must overcome yourself to see the Child-King."

Melchior smiled at the answer, for he knew that his servant Jewel was correct. Then Jewel added,

"And when you see the Child-King, you'll see something that every other believer on earth will yearn to see."

The three magi looked at Jewel for he didn't tell them what they would see. Jewel smiled, then said with finality,

"You'll see with your eye the King of Kings."

9

ENTERING THE MYSTERY CIRCLE ROOM

Melchior is a Circle-Maker

The three magi finished their lunch. Balthazar and Gaspar did most of the talking about the spectacular star and what they knew about it. Melchior could tell from their attitude that they were proud of their knowledge. Melchior felt they knew enough to go into his Circle Room, but they were arrogant in their ignorance. Melchior abruptly stood and spoke sharply, as though he were a teacher rebuking an erring student.

"Gentlemen, I've heard you speak of different stars, but you don't speak with precision . . ." He let his words trail off so that what he said could sink in.

"You, Balthazar, you talk of Orion and the bands stars, called the three kings. You describe them with deep passion as one describes a beautiful woman, or sumptuous roasted meat—all seasoned, cooked to perfection."

Melchior waited before continuing. "I congratulate your passion for the stars—the passion of Ethiopia—but the Persian mind is more analytical, more demanding, more exact."

"NO! . . .," an embarrassed Balthazar stood up next to his host, Melchior. "I appreciate your hospitality, but I do not appreciate your rudeness."

"Shh . . .," Melchior put a finger to his lips. "I spoke not to embarrass you, but to point out the different strengths each of us have about the stars. In a few minutes I will take you into the Circle Room. In that room you will see an instrument that I use to measure the movement of the stars. I can tell you when they speed up, and I can tell you when they move closer to our earth, or they move away. I will show you the charts of my analytical examination of the stars. When you see the map of the heavens . . . and when you enter the Circle Room, then . . . then . . . your mind will be challenged as never before. I will show you some precise calculations about the stars that the world has never seen. I have discovered movements among the stars that no magi has ever conceived. What I have found is world-changing."

Melchior then smiled, as though looking for Balthazar's agreement. But the Ethiopian did not return the smile. He was skeptical, Melchior's claims seem exaggerated to him. Balthazar needed more proof from his host before he would smile.

But Gaspar, the magi from Europe, at least nodded in agreement. The Europeans had analytical minds, so Gaspar understood what Melchior was proposing.

Then Melchior turned to Gaspar, the magi from the West, "Everyone knows your Western mind is guarded by a strong, indomitable will. Your power of choice controls the way the Western mind thinks, and the things you think. Your will can turn off your mind, or your will can turn on your thoughts."

Melchior smiled at younger Gaspar; it was a knowing smile. "I know the Persians are more scientific than the Africans, and so do you."

Melchior smiled.

Gaspar smiled.

Finally, Balthazar smiled.

"Together, we can discover new messages from the stars that the Persian astronomer alone—like himself—cannot discover."

"Together . . . we can discover new directions that we should take, that the Ethiopian astronomer with all his passion could not discover alone.

"Together . . . we can unlock the mystery of God that the Western astronomer could not discover without the aid of the Eastern mind, or the African mind.

"But together we will examine the charts of past movements of the stars. We will be able to determine if there has ever been a star in the west. We will find out if there was a past star in the west that could have exploded, creating the spectacular bright star we saw the other night. If we find there was never a star in the western sky, then we will know the star we saw was supernatural."

The three men stood facing each other, not speaking for a long time—their eyes never meeting. They were looking deep within the souls of one another. They couldn't say Melchior was wrong. Each was putting the pieces of the puzzle together in his mind.

"Come . . .," demanded Melchior with a touch of mystery.

He led them to the door to the Circle Room, only one door to the room that was always locked. The large metal-green key was inserted, and the tumblers fell into place with an eerie "*CLICK.*" The door swung open to pitch black darkness.

"We'll need some candles," the host suggested. The two guests of Melchior stared in through the door, but saw nothing . . . nothing. Empty blackness stared back at them.

Light over their shoulders seeped into the dark room; slowly the two guests began to perceive some tall, folded charts leaning against a wall, and tall, thin boxes leaning against another wall. High boxes. Too tall to sit on. Too narrow to be a seat or table. As their eyes dilated, they could see there were no tops on the boxes. There were holes, many holes, in the top of the boxes. They could see rolled-up charts in the many holes in the boxes.

"Let's hold the candle high," Melchior spoke.

The three men entered a small Circle Room that Melchior

explained was a basement to a Circle Room above them. "This room is where I keep the charts."

"What's on the charts?" the inquisitive Gaspar asked.

"It's easier to show you one chart than explain my system." Melchior pulled one long chart out of the box where it was carefully stored.

"Let's roll out this chart on the long table. I want to show you how one star travels across the heavens."

The table was extremely long, long enough to seat twelve people on each side, yet narrow, only a couple of feet wide. It was a table Melchior had built so he could roll out the charts for study.

"On this table I study the travel of stars and record it on these charts."

When Gaspar first saw the table, he thought to himself why it was so narrow. *There's not enough room for people to eat.* When Melchior explained about the charts, he understood.

The chart was rolled to the exact length of the table. "I have these special scrolls made from the finest vellum-calf skin . . . they are made for this table."

Balthazar spoke up, "You make the charts the length of the table," then laughed as a man with great insight.

"No . . .," Melchior quietly corrected Balthazar, with a touch of arrogance. "The charts are cut to the exact length of the Circle Room upstairs. That's the room you haven't seen yet."

"I don't understand," Balthazar queried.

"You will in time," Melchior continued with his all-knowing smile. The old Persian was like a little boy, showing off his latest trick to some friends. Melchior was the center of attention; it was a place he enjoyed. And this center of attention involved showing off his erudite knowledge, which meant he enjoyed being recognized for his brilliance. It was important to Melchior for people to think he was intelligent.

As the chart was unrolled, it showed long curving lines drawn on the chart from one end of the table to the other. Each curve was identical to the others, removed by only the narrowest of space. But it was easy to tell the curving lines apart by the color of ink. Each line became progressively lighter from the top of the chart to the bottom of the chart. Melchior explained:

"I mix the ink to a different component each night to show the difference between the lines," Melchior explained. "Actually, Jewel mixes the ink for me." Then Melchior digressed from the topic of the lines to explain about the ink.

"Jewel has been mixing ink since he was a little boy in rabbinical school when he was in the Holy Land. He makes ink for me from the same type of charcoal—made from cedar wood— that he made in the Holy Land. He crushes the charcoal into a fine powder, then mixes it with olive oil. He uses the oil from a red olive grown a few miles from here. The red olive turns brownish-black when crushed. It makes brown-black ink."

Melchior loved the authority he felt when teaching anything. "Each week Jewel adds a different amount of olive oil to the crushed charcoal to get a different shade. I can tell the different trajectories of a star as it travels each week by the color of the ink."

The house guests, Balthazar and Gaspar, were impressed. Melchior could see it in their eyes that they were learning. An enlightened student always gave him satisfaction.

"I also have written numbers on each curving line to tell the different weeks when a star makes its journey across the sky." Melchior walked the length of the long table pointing to dates when the star on that chart had made its journey. "This chart proves that stars travel across the heavens, but they follow a different path each day. I can't measure days with my charts, but I can measure different weeks."

Then Melchior's voice grew in confidence. "I can prove stars travel, but they always travel a different path."

Melchior pointed to a very narrow door in the ceiling, a very small door. He explained, "That door is very small because the other side of the door is the floor on which I write. Come, I'll explain."

Melchior lifted the door up into the Circle Room, then placed the candle into the room. The old man—creaking bones and all—carefully crawled up through the small door into the room. The floor of the Circle Room was the bottom of a sphere or ball. As Melchior slipped into the room, he slid down an incline to the bottom of the room. Then, yelling out to his two friends, Melchior announced,

"This room—the Circle Room—is a giant sphere. When you enter, it's like crawling into a giant ball." Melchior held the candle high; Balthazar looked in through the door, peering at the round sides of the Circle Room. Gaspar, looking over his shoulder, didn't say anything—he only gawked at the Circle Room. He had never seen anything like it in his life.

"Come on in . . . slide down to the bottom of the ball."

The two friends stood back to back at the bottom of the sphere. They were staring at the inside of a ball. Its walls were painted black because black surface absorbed any light of the flickering candle. The magi could barely make out the round walls.

"There's an opening at the very top of the room," Melchior explained. "It's covered in the daylight, but at night I open the hole to study the stars."

"Why a circle room?" Gaspar asked the older Melchior. "I've never seen one like this anywhere. I've never even heard of a room like this."

Melchior smiled at the response, and he was glad Gaspar said he'd never heard of a perfectly-round, circular room. The orange candlelight revealed a slight smile on the old Persian's face. He spoke:

"There's not another chart room like this anywhere. I thought it up, and I've never told anyone about this room. I don't want other magi to find out what I know. No one has ever been in this room. Today you are the first outsiders to see this room and enter it. Tonight, you'll be the first to help me in my scientific surveys."

Balthazar and Gaspar still hadn't said anything. They were busy surveying the curved walls; they hadn't come to the question yet—"Why?" They were still struggling with the "What's here?" question.

Gaspar climbed on hands and knees up one side of the inner ball, almost to the halfway mark. He slowly smoothed his hand over the surface. He rapped on the plaster coating with a knuckle. Then he asked a simple question,

"Why so hard?"

"Because I have to write on the charts that I lay out on these walls," Melchior let his statement sink in. He waited until his two friends finished examining the room—there wasn't much to see besides a tiny hole in the ceiling and the small narrow door through which they entered. The oldest magi waited until he had their full attention. Then Melchior explained,

"The charts are all the identical length of half this room." Melchior pointed from one side of the inner ball to the other. "I cover the inside of the circular room with charts, then I draw a line of each star from one end of the chart to the other. I can trace the travel of a star each night from one end of the chart to the other. Life is not a straight line; life is a circle, and I have discovered our universe is a circle. The moon and stars disappear in the west with the coming of each new morning. Then they reappear each evening to travel across the sky."

The round Circle Room in the middle of the round chantry was constructed in the shape of the universe. Melchior told his two friends what they already knew, "All the stars that disappear over the western horizon eventually come back the following night on the eastern horizon."

The analytical Gaspar asked, "Does that mean we live in the center of the universe, and all the stars travel around us?"

Melchior answered the penetrating question with another question, "The opposite could be true. Could our earth spin on an axis and the stars be stationary?"

"Whatever answer we choose, it means our earth is round, a heretical belief in this day. The other magi would think I'm crazy; that's why I've told no one about this room."

"Ah!" commented Gaspar. "You are making our earth into a circle. Not a flat surface."

"Ha, Ha, Ha . . ." the outspoken Ethiopian magi filled the Circle Room with laughter. "Melchior makes the universe a circle, just like he's made this Circle Room. He's the Circle-Maker!"

"Yes," Melchior accepted the compliment. "But just as the stars travel from East to West, some stars confuse me as they shoot toward the East." He called them "shooting stars." He didn't know the names of the comets, but he had drawn them on his charts as they moved in different directions from the majority of the stars.

"But the majority of the stars move from East to West. The other magi think the stars move in a straight line. But if that happened, then stars would be the same as God." Melchior answered.

Then the Persian continued, "To move in a straight line—without end—is to move in a straight line forever; they would not come back the following night."

"But the stars do come back," Gaspar added.

Melchior continued, "If stars traveled straight, without turning, they'd be like God. They would be infinite, which means they would be 'without limits.'"

Melchior continued his explanation, "Space is the distance between objects, and when you come to the last object in the universe—in this case—you come to the last jump out into nothingness. Somewhere the stars end, for if the stars didn't end, they would be limitless; they would be as big as God."

Melchior continued, "Only God is without limits; He knows all things knowable. He has all power to do all things that are doable. If all things revolve around the earth, and all things revolve around God, then the earth is special to God."

Melchior pointed to the small hole in the very top of the "ball" room. There was a small dot in the center of that small circle held in place by wires. Melchior explained further thoughts about a straight line.

"I line up a straight line from a star through that dot in the ceiling to a point on my chart." Melchior elaborated that it took three points to make a mark on a chart: from the star, through the dot in the hole in the ceiling, to an exact point on the floor. Then he marked that spot on the chart that was laid out on the inside of the ball.

"How do you know you have the exact spot on the floor?" the inquisitive Balthazar asked.

"Ah . . ., that's a good question," Melchior responded. He pulled a thin metal sheet of bronze out of his pocket. It had a small hole in the metal. "When the hole in this metal sheet lines up with the hole in the ceiling and the star, I make a mark."

Melchior explained that a star didn't travel the same route across the sky each evening, but followed a different path—the same direction and the same speed—but each night the path was a little different from the night before. Then the old Persian boasted:

"The other magi draw their charts from their imagination, but their charts are not as accurate as mine. They guess how far apart to draw the paths on their charts, but mine are accurate. I draw each star where they are located."

Suddenly, without an explanation, both Balthazar and Gaspar understood why the lines in Melchior's charts were different colors, and why each different color was numbered. The wise old Melchior continued,

"I've drawn several stars on the same chart: that's because they are near each other in the sky." Then Melchior wistfully said,

"I wish I had some way to measure the brightness of their light; some stars are much brighter than others."

For the next few minutes the three fellow-magi sat in the bottom of the circle ball, talking about the intensity of the stars. They had various theories why some stars are brighter than others and why a particular star may be brighter in the early night, while another star was brighter toward morning. Then the three magi stopped talking. Their fertile minds were still thinking about their unanswered questions. Old Melchior interrupted the silence,

"Come, I want to show you one particular night. I'll get the chart out of the box and spread one night before you. Then you can tell me what you think."

Melchior climbed out of the room through the narrow door, then retrieved the chart for the 25th day of the 12th month. He carefully checked the number and handed it to his two friends. The numbers on the chart was in bold, black ink. As the two magi spread the chart on the inside of the ball floor, they noticed the chart was worn and frayed at the edges. When Melchior realized they were examining the edges he answered their inner questions even before they asked,

"'I've looked at this chart many more times than the others."

The chart was finally in place. Melchior smiled because he knew what dates were recorded in the corner of the chart. With some amusement, Melchior let the magi trace the stars to find out their names. Balthazar finally exclaimed loudly,

"There's Orion . . . ."

And Gaspar immediately interrupted, "And these are the three belt stars in a perfect line."

"This chart is the 25th day of the last month of the year."

Quickly, Gaspar carefully traced the line on the chart to examine the three belt stars. He ran his fingers from one star, to the other star, to the third star.

"The three belt stars are in an exact straight line," Gaspar announced innocently. "Are you sure the line is straight?" Gaspar confessed he had often questioned what he saw in the winter night. He had often wondered if the line between them was, in fact, perfectly straight. Gaspar didn't know what "perfectly straight" meant, but he knew it was special.

"Perfectly straight," Melchior answered his two friends.

"What does that mean," Gaspar finally verbalized his question.

Balthazar shook his head negatively. He had seen the straight line, but to emotional people, a straight line was not the source of a question. To Balthazar, a straight line meant it was not bent.

Melchior answered, "Since only God can draw a straight line from eternity to eternity, then God is trying to tell us something with this straight line between the belt stars."

Then Melchior asked the question that would later be answered for them,

"Is God telling us He's doing something special on the 25th day of the 12th month?"

Melchior began searching for more charts. He was searching all the charts for the 25th day of the 12th month. He stretched each one out across the long table.

"Not here . . .," Melchior said after examining each chart.

Both Balthazar and Gaspar knew what the wily old astronaut was doing. He was searching for any trace of the spectacular star they saw on the 25th day. It was not there!

"Could you have missed it?" Balthazar asked.

"No . . .," The old magi was angered at the suggestion he was not a through observer. "To miss the sensational star is like missing the setting sun that ends a beautiful day."

They all examined the charts for the 25th day. There was no indication the star had previously appeared. They all were coming to the conclusion that the star was a once-in-a-lifetime event.

But more than the appearance of the spectacular star, they were beginning to realize God had shown them the star for a purpose.

Each man was sitting in his own silence when Jewel interrupted the quiet moment,

"Tea time . . .," a voice from the outside drifted into the chart room. It was Jewel announcing,

"You will get deeper insight into the stars when you brighten your minds with some tea."

10

PREPARING FOR A LIFE-CHANGING JOURNEY

....

What Shall We Give the Baby-King?

Melchior asked his two friends, "How does one pack for a journey of 1,200 miles? What does one take? Considering 'camel travel,' what does one leave behind?"

Balthazar suggested,

"The wisest answer is to consider the goal of our trip. We're going to see a person—the Child-King—and you may be in His presence for only a few moments. We must consider the gift that we will give the King."

Melchior walked over to the stone floor surrounding the crackling fire. He was holding a long steel bar in his hand. One of his magi friends asked,

"Are you carrying that steel rod for protection, or will it be the scepter for your kingdom?"

Melchior smiled, but ignored the comment. He tapped the steel bar on each stone, hearing a "THUD." Then the right stone gave a hollow ring, "Thoood."

The old Persian's eyes gleamed with anticipation, "Ah . . . it is still here." Melchior handed the bar to Jewel, directing him to remove some stones from the floor. "Thump . . . thump . . . thump!"

The servant broke mortar holding the stones in place, then pried the heavy stones out of the ground. When the stones were gone, Melchior reached into the shallow hole to begin scooping away sand with his hands. He had the happy anticipation of a child playing in the yard. Then everyone heard it at the same time,

"Scra-a-a-a-p . . . scra-a-a-a-p . . ."

Melchior's hands scraped the top of a metal box. Everyone knew immediately what he was doing. Melchior was getting his treasure to give to the Child-King.

Lifting the metal container from the hole, his old eyes twinkling, Melchior blew away the dry sand. Balthazar asked,

"Where's the key . . .?"

Melchior looked up into his eyes and playfully chided his Ethiopian friend,

"A key couldn't keep my treasure safe, if the thief stole the whole box."

With shaking fingers—Melchior had done more physical activity than he should—he carefully lifted the lid. Everyone saw at the same time a pile of old dust-covered coins, corroded with time.

"These coins will shine with a little polish," Melchior's voice broke the silent investigation of inquiring eyes. "These gold coins will sparkle when I give them to the Child-King."

Melchior explained the tradition in the Near East. "When a baby is born to a king—the baby boy who is in line to be the next king—all neighboring kings would bring a gift of gold to the newborn king."

"A gift of gold insured peace between the Baby-King and the kingdom presenting the gold."

Jewel remarked, "I didn't know this gold was here." Then he added, "These coins are more valuable than money!" The other two magi nodded their heads in agreement. "There's more wealth in these gold coins than any rich man can possess." Again the two magi nodded approval.

"Why didn't you tell me about it?" Jewel asked. "I wouldn't have told anyone."

Melchior smiled with his response, "No one can tell another my secret if I don't tell it to them."

Then Melchior explained that the gold coins were passed from father to son for twelve generations. The coins came from the treasury of King Gaumata, his grandfather twelve generations ago. He ruled Persia when the magi were in power. Melchior continued,

"These coins have the likeness of Gaumata and the inscription, 'Magi Rule.' Yes, these coins are valuable because they are gold, but they are more valuable than a historic treasure." Melchior stopped talking, then began to tear up, and his voice quivered.

"These gold coins will make the baby the next king!"

The two friends saw tears in Melchior's eyes. He struggled to put words to his emotions. A cough or two, then the old patriarch spoke through broken words,

"These coins prove my right to the Persian throne." Then Melchior told how his father said to him—what each father passed on to his son—that when the stars in heaven were right, the son with these coins would use this treasure to become king. These gold coins were Melchior's key to the kingdom.

"But now I will need these coins no longer." As Melchior spoke, Jewel and the two magi realized they were sensing deep conviction. Melchior continued,

"I will offer these coins to the Child-King. I will give my right to the throne to Immanuel—God with us. He will be king."

Later that day, Balthazar came into the kitchen where the other two magi were getting ready for the trip. The Ethiopian magi placed a box on the table in front of them, saying,

"I, too, have a gift to offer the young king." He slowly opened the lid; any swift movement would have created a breeze, and any small movement of air would have blown away the reddish powder. Balthazar answered,

"It's frankincense . . . ." "I've given deep thought to what gift I should give the Boy-King. Since I read the Deliverer would be more than a ruling King—he would be a Priest—my gift will be frankincense, used by priests in their worship of God."

All three magi knew that frankincense was burned in worship. Its sweet smell transformed the stale air of any house—including a temple—into a delightful meadow, a desirable place to live.

A rich king had frankincense sprinkled throughout his palace to please him, no matter what room he entered. In the Near East frankincense was burned in temple to worship the richness of God and to invite God into the presence of worshipers. A temple is a house where God lived, and God will come live when He is honored.

Balthazar reminded them, "The burning of incense is like our prayers going up to God. When we mix frankincense with our prayers, God will answer."

Balthazar carefully put the lid on the box so no powder would escape, but the fragrance of the perfume remained in the air. He commented, "If it smells so wonderful when the top is removed, think how much more wonderful it will smell when burned and its incense is mixed with prayers."

Then Balthazar added, "I will give frankincense to the Priest-King because He will bring spiritual peace to the world. The struggle of mankind against evil will end when the Priest-King rules the earth."

Gaspar was not to be outdone. He left the kitchen, but returned quickly with an exquisite urn. "This will be my gift to the virgin-born King."

Gaspar said he had read the Isaiah scroll again more carefully. "I found the King will also be a suffering Messiah." He unrolled his scroll to the correct spot, "Listen to how Isaiah describes the King Messiah,"

"He was despised, and no one cared,
He carried our weaknesses,
He bore our sorrows;
He was wounded for our transgressions,
He was crushed for our sins.
He was punished for our crimes against God;
By His stripes we are healed.
We are like sheep, all have strayed from God;
Each of us has turned to our own way,
Yet the Lord laid on Him the guilt of all.
He was oppressed, yet He was submissive;
He did not open His mouth when punished.
Like a lamb led to be slaughtered,
Like a sheep before its shearers,
He did not open His mouth.
He was taken from prison
He was tried and taken away to His death;
No one realized He was dying for their sins
That He was suffering their punishment.
He had never done any wrong,
He never deceived anyone.
He was buried like a criminal
In a rich man's grave"
(Isa. 53:3-9).

The magi listened carefully to the predictions of Isaiah. They had rejoiced in the coming King who ushered in peace, where the lion lies down with the lamb. But the suffering of the Messiah-King troubled them.

"What does it mean?" Balthazar asked.

"All I know," Melchior answered, "is that when the magi ruled Persia, the nation enjoyed a kingdom of spiritual peace. Then a murderer killed my great-grandfather. Perhaps someone will murder the Child-King."

Balthazar then commented, "Yes, evil men will probably kill the Child-King."

Then the Ethiopian quoted a Greek scholar,

"Socrates said, 'If a perfect man ever lives, the world would kill him.'"

The three magi were saddened by their thoughts. But Jewel, who knew better, wanted to tell them what happened after the death of the Child-King. Jewel knew what would happen after He was buried. He knew what the word *peace* meant, but he was not allowed to speak.

Gaspar turned their attention to his gift. "This urn is filled with myrrh, the ointment of healing and health. If the Messiah-King is to be beaten, He will need myrrh to soothe His wounds."

Gaspar explained that myrrh could mean healing for crimes of evil men. Myrrh could mean health for mankind and bring in a millennium of peace.

Gaspar said, "Myrrh is special to me; it comes from the dried sap of the Commiphora bush or tree. The stem must be "wounded" like the messiah King will be wounded. The white healing sap drips from the tree's wounds and is gathered for healing."

"Just as Jewel must crush the tea leaves to give its life more abundantly to those who drink, so the enjoyment of life comes from death. So, the 'wounds' of the tree must produce death to gives us life more abundantly."

Then Gaspar explained, "Just as Melchior's gift of gold represents His inheritance of the throne, and Balthazar's gift of frankincense represents His priestly duties, I'll take the Child-King that flask of myrrh to show my love for His suffering."

The next day the three future kings left the chantry to embark on the journey of a lifetime. Three camels were packed, kneeling and waiting at the door of the round home. The fourth camel would be ridden by Jewel who would guide a pack animal with their supplies.

"Should we ask for armed soldiers to guard us on our travels?"

Melchior asked as the three approached their beast of burden. "We have expensive gifts; evil men could rob and beat us for them."

"No," Jewel had thought of everything. "If we take soldiers, the Romans will think we are an expeditionary force. They might attack us or at least arrest us. Then we could be captives. Your turban will tell everyone you are magi. Everyone knows the magi are men of peace."

"What about thieves?"

"No . . .," Jewel had an explanation. "thieves will be afraid to harm you. They know the magi have power with the stars. They will be afraid we might curse them."

"But . . .," Melchior confessed, "we magi know our power is in our knowledge. We do not have powers of superstition . . . and incantations . . . and potions. That is an old-wives tale."

"Yes," answered Jewel. "You know that, but the common people don't know that. They are afraid of you."

Melchior was still cautious. He was afraid that some tribes on the other side of the Euphrates did not know the tradition of magi. "Suppose a tribe is ignorant of our reputation? Suppose they come kill us?"

"No," again Jewel spoke in defense of the trip, "we go to worship the Child-King. The LORD in heaven who has sent His Son to be born by a miracle of a virgin—He will protect us. If the LORD of heaven has power to send His Son to come live among us, He has power to protect us."

"But . . ., if . . .,"

"No," Jewel answered more strongly than a servant should answer. But Jewel was answering with faith in God. "We must have faith in the LORD of heaven to protect us on our pilgrimage—a journey that He has shown us by the star."

Jewel's words were more convincing than those of a mere human man. He spoke with the authority of God. The three magi listened to Jewel and took confidence in Jewel's faith. They mounted their camels and turned West.

MELCHIOR - TEMPTED TO THE CROWN OF PERSIA

···

A Choice Against the Passion of Position

Jewel led the three camels on the road built by Darius, king of Persia, from Persepelis to Sosa to Ecbatana. The three magi were still traveling in Persia. A cold winter wind snapped the tunic around Jewel's legs. He yelled back to the three magi,

"Don't worry, this wind will die down when the sun sets. It'll be a cold night, but there won't be any snow."

"How do you know?" Balthazar yelled back through the piercing wind.

"I just know . . . ."

The tea kettle sizzled above the fire that Jewel just built. Tea was always the first item on the agenda when making camp. Just as Jewel predicted, there was no wind, only bone-chilling cold. It was a bitter night. Each bundled as tightly as possible and huddled close to the fire.

"I chose this spot because there is a lot of wood available, and we will be protected through the night," Jewel said in a matter-of-fact way.

"*WHAT'S THAT?*" Balthazar was the first to hear the approach of thundering horses' hoofs through the silent night. Riders were coming fast and approaching quickly. "That's not a traveler; that must be one of the king's messengers," Melchior said. He knew that government messengers rode swift horses to connect quickly to all points in the kingdom. The fire was burning low, and the riders were interrupting the magi's preparation for sleep.

The horses were jerked to a stop at the encampment. Yes, they were the king's messengers, dressed in partial battle gear.

"Hmmm," Melchior thought, *their leader is Commander from my home town. Why is he sent as a messenger? He's too important to deliver messages.*

Jewel put extra wood on the fire to provide light. Commander walked into the camp. His hand was not on his weapon; he was coming in peace. Commander looked through the dark; his eyes were not adjusted to the light. He blinked and announced,

"Are you the ones I am looking for?" Then he went on to explain, "I am sent to find the three magi who are journeying to the land of Palestine."

Jewel spoke up quickly to tell Commander the identity of the three magi. "The first is Melchior from the line of the royal Persian family of 400 years ago. Second is Balthazar from the line of the king in Ethiopia. And third is Gaspar from the line of the king of Tarshish, a protectorate of Spain.

"I am only looking for Melchior, the Persian magi who lives in the circle chantry." Commander was smiling, a grin of good news. Previously, Commander had brought bad news of taxes.

"I've paid my taxes," Melchior quickly spoke up. "I've done nothing wrong."

Commander laughed with a smile of approval. "The king has sent me with a wonderful message for you, Melchior. You've not done anything wrong. The king sent me to deliver this message because I knew you and would recognize you." He also knew you would trust my word." Commander didn't want to mention that Melchior–from the Gaumata family line–would get a promotion. And that he too was from that family.

Commander dug into an expensive pouch hanging around his shoulder to retrieve a small scroll. Melchior could see that the scroll was vellum leather, an expensive scroll. Then Commander saluted, showing reverence to Melchior, and then with a bowed head showing further reverence, he knelt and handed the scroll to Melchior with both hands.

The other two magi were wide-eyed at the reverence showed the ancient Melchior. But they were careful not to comment and intrude upon the moment.

Melchior moved over to the firelight, then began to read the scroll. He was excited inwardly but not outwardly so anyone could tell. It read,

To Melchior, the magian. I know you helped me settle a growing revolt of the magi against the taxes on their chantry. Many of my advisers were afraid of sorcery and incantations against them by some of the magi. The governor of your province has been removed from his office. I am looking for a replacement.

Because you have royal blood flowing in your veins, and because of the great wisdom given to you by the gods, and because of your ability to bring our people together; I invite you to return to my palace as quickly as possible. I want you to advise me who should be the next governor, or I want to nominate you as the next governor of your province. If you refuse my offer, you must know of someone as wise as you who can become the next governor.

Written this first day of November; sealed with my seal

Melchior rolled up the scroll and tucked it in an inner pocket. He would keep this prize the rest of his life. Finally, someone recognized Gaumata family blood flowing in his veins. Thoughts raced through his head, bumping into one another. He found himself unable to think logically for the first time in his life.

A few hours ago, he was willing to go through any tortured weather to locate the Baby- King. He planned to ford all rivers and to do whatever possible to find and worship the Baby-King. He was more resolved than at any time in his life to even die to fulfill this impossible dream.

But now, the scroll held greater possibilities than the previous impossible dream. He never believed he would become a leader in Persia, or possibly the king of Persia. Yet it was something he wanted with all his strength. Now this scroll could be a door–an open door–that could lead to the throne of Persia.

Melchior thought to himself, *I was born the son of a king. But was I predestined to be king? Is this the opportunity to become a king?*

Melchior was wise not to tell what was in the scroll. Gaspar and Balthazar didn't ask. They knew it was important because of the way Commander presented it. But finally their curiosity got the best of them. Balthazar blurted out, "What was in the scroll?"

"Some messages should not be revealed before their time."

The other two wishful kings understood the importance of the metaphor, so they didn't ask again. Turning to the two soldiers, Melchior said,

"Commander . . . there is much wood in this place. You can camp near us for the night. My servant tells me it will not snow tonight, nor will the wind return. Tomorrow morning, we will talk about the message in the scroll."

Balthazar snored loudly when he slept, and the louder he snored, the deeper he slept. That night, his blankets kept him warm, and the snoring was heard by the soldiers who were camped a distance away. Gaspar didn't snore; he just slept.

But not Melchior. In a moment, he was ready to turn his camel around to follow Commander back to the king's palace. Tomorrow could be a new day, a golden day. Tomorrow could lead to a golden crown. Melchior even thought of how the crown would fit on his head. He looked in the mirror of his mind and saw the crown on his thin gray hair. Then he smiled in approval of what he saw.

But the night was cold, and his blanket was not comfortable. He tossed from one side to the other. He thought about the Hebrew scrolls and the prophecy of the future Redeemer of the Jews . . . and the world. *The star . . . I cannot deny what I saw. Does the star announce the coming of the King who is to rule the world? He's been born in the West. I must go and worship Him.*

Melchior wrestled with the ground; his was a dream of being the king of Persia, versus the dream of worshipping the King who would rule the world. In the darkness, a spiritual struggle went on between a demon of pride, wrestling against an angel from God. All night long, they wrestled.

The sun came up cloudless in the East, a cold morning without wind. No sign of a storm on any horizon. Melchior had not slept all night, but he finally concluded, *I would rather worship the King who will rule the world than be an earthly king who would rule only a few years over one of the nations of the world.* And with that small surrender of his lifelong dream, Melchior finally went to sleep for an hour. He slept soundly until awakened by Jewel.

"Hot tea . . .?"

Commander came to sit next to Jewel's fire. He left his soldiers at their camp; his conversation was private for Melchior. Commander asked the two magi and Jewel to leave them. Intimate messages from the heart are delivered in private.

"The king has great confidence in you," Commander told Melchior what he already knew. "When you become the governing leader of our providence, you are only a heartbeat away from the throne."

Commander told him that many of the king's counselors

respected Melchior. They would look to him if the king were to die. Then Commander looked deep into Melchior's soul to ask,

"Do the stars predict the return of a Gaumata to the throne?" Commander also had Gaumata's blood flowing in his veins, but he was a realist. The strong military soldier knew he didn't have a chance at becoming king, but this could be a once-in-a-lifetime opportunity to the throne. *This is an open door waiting for your grand entrance.*

Melchior had gone up to the top of the hill to think, to clear his thoughts.

The sun had been up for about two hours. Melchior stood next to his camel. In a few moments Jewel would tap the front knees of the camel for it to bend down to receive its rider.

Commander had saddled his white stallion, gripping the reins, fearful that Melchior would say "no." He didn't want to deliver a negative to the king. No one spoke; it was a sacred moment felt by all. Melchior looked toward the western horizon where the star had been seen. Then he turned back to look into the sun rising in the east. Finally he broke the silence,

"Commander, thank you for your diligent pursuit of us, and thank you for your craftiness to find us. I have a message to give to your king. Listen carefully to repeat exactly what I say to you, for each word that I speak comes from a king to my king. What I say represents the truth of the ages.

"I would long to come serve the king of Persia because I am Persian born. One day I will be buried in a Persian grave. I believe being a Persian king is the greatest power on earth. But tell your king, I saw a spectacular star in the western sky that had never been there before. These magi with me also saw the heavenly star. We believe it was a sign from God that He would send His Son to earth. I believe in the star, and the Child to whom it pointed. The vision of that star has guided me to this very spot on my journey. I will go to the Holy Land to take gifts to the One who is born King of the earth. You know the tradition of the

Gautama coins. The one who has those coins will be guaranteed the crown. I will give these coins to heaven's Baby. These kingly coins are my gift to the newborn King. He will rule the world, and we will live in peace. There will be no wars between nations, and soldiers like you, Commander, will not be needed to keep peace. There will be no lying or disease. A lion and the lamb will lie down together. Children will play with deadly snakes and not be hurt. I must follow the leading of my star to worship this King, and perhaps in some small way, I can serve Him."

1 2

FROM EAST TO WEST: CROSSING THE EUPHRATES

....

The Threshold between Two Cultures

The three magi astride their camels looked down on a wide sandy valley in front of them. The hills on either side of the valley were soft and low, but the river in the valley was threatening. Crossing the valley is easy; crossing the Euphrates is perilous.

The Euphrates, a treacherous green snake winding back and forth, crawled through the brown sandy valley, separating the East from the West. It took over a half day of camel travel to reach its banks from the time they first sighted the dividing line between East and West.

Deep . . . wide . . . and rushing, the Euphrates was apparently uncrossable to all. "If we had followed a trail, we would have found a ferry," complained Balthazar, who had experienced desert traveling.

"There's a wide spot about five miles upriver," commented Jewel. "It's shallow enough to cross, and the bottom has small pebbles; it's easy to cross them."

"How do you know this?" The inquisitive Gaspar asked what all three were thinking.

"A servant must know these things." Jewel didn't get specific. "And I remember what I hear."

When the entourage reached the ford, it was shallower

than Jewel described; the water sloshed around the camel's knees. Then Balthazar suggested, "Let's eat before we cross the river; the food will give us strength in case we face an emergency."

"No, let's eat after we cross," Gaspar suggested. "We'll enjoy our food more—and we can rest. Doing the hard thing first will make the easier task more enjoyable. Our meal will be more enjoyment on the other side. Then we can rest there."

"Alright," said Balthazar, shrugging his shoulders.

The crossing was uneventful, other than dodging some floating debris. On the other side, Jewel spread out a blanket and opened a cloth sack of fruit. Then he passed out strips of dried meat. The three magi lay snoozing in the afternoon sun, their wet leggings quickly drying in the warm breeze.

The magi hadn't noticed Jewel had built a small fire, and there perched on the rocks was his ever-present tea kettle. Soon the shrill of its whistle awakened the magi. As they were stretching away their aches, Jewel announced,

"Tea time . . . ."

The men sat facing the Euphrates, and Melchior noted, "This river is world famous; even the Hebrew Scripture says the Euphrates flowed through the Garden of Eden." Melchior believed the Euphrates was the first river created by God.

Then Gaspar commented, "You remember, I'm from the West, I'm glad to be back on the west side of the Euphrates." When he said that, he remembered Melchior had never been this far from his home. So he asked Melchior, "How does it feel to travel this far from home and to cross into a different world?"

Melchior thought before answering, and his two friends didn't fill the quiet space with talking. They waited for his answer; they really wanted to know his feelings.

"East men think like men of the East,
West men think like men of the West;
Yet, men on both sides think alike.
Men of the East think—might makes right,
While men of the West think—right makes might.
It's not the Euphrates that makes them think differently,
It's what's on the inside of a man that makes him think differently.
It's the way men think that separates the East from the West."

Gaspar, the man from the East, had a question, "What do you mean men of the East think might makes right?"

Melchior pointed out, "The armies of the East and West fight differently; it's not their muscles or strength that wins a battle; it's their discipline in fighting. The Parthians of the East are vicious in battle, and they fight with all their emotions, throwing themselves into conflict to destroy or be destroyed. They rampage . . . they pillage . . . they rape . . . they torture."

Balthazar and Gaspar nodded in agreement; they knew about men of the East in battle, and they had heard the stories.

Melchior then added, "The Romans, men of the West, are men of the law; they have written the greatest code of laws ever devised by mankind. In battle a Roman soldier obeys orders, they fight in disciplined units, they protect one another. They never fight like the Parthians to destroy or maim. The Romans fight to conquer and rule by law. If they lose a battle, their discipline demands they retreat and formulate a new plan and a new strategy. They plan to fight another day. Their concept of right dictates how they fight.

Then Melchior pointed to his two friends to make his point, "The Romans did not destroy you but took you prisoner to be sold as slaves. Their enemies are not pillaged, or raped, or destroyed. Their discipline controls their actions."

Then Melchior pointed out what they must do when

they reach Jerusalem and face both Jews and Romans. "When we face the Romans, we must not think like magi from the East; it's not our might that will prevail. We must think like men of the West; we must use their strength against them. For in every strength there is weakness, just as there is weakness in every strength.

"Because the men of the West are men of the law, we must appeal to their law; we must use their law to make them want to help us. We will be their superiors by allowing them to help us find the Child-King."

After the afternoon meal, the entourage discussed their next move. Gaspar suggested, "If we follow the path of many stars we see every night, we'll go straight across the desert toward Jerusalem."

"*NO!*" Jewel shouted, "*NO . . . NO . . . NO!*" The servant was adamant. "We will die if we cross the desert."

Jewel explained a straight path was over 800 miles of sand and desert. There were no villages to find food and no oasis to find water and no paths to follow. They would wander aimlessly in the desert. There would be steep cliffs they couldn't climb; they'd have to re-trace their paths. They would get lost in box canyons. They would die in the desert. Then Jewel concluded,

"No travelers ever cross the desert; only those who live in the desert know the ways of the desert."

"How do you know these dangers?" Gaspar asked. "You have not crossed the desert; you are not from around here."

"I know because it's my duty to know," was all Jewel said. "I know because it's a servant's task to guide his master safely."

Melchior, who had known Jewel longest, suspected Jewel knew more than he was saying. But since Jewel had been right on other occasions, Melchior decided to support him now. The wise elderly Melchior asked,

"Jewel, how should we travel to Jerusalem?"

"We will follow the road on the eastern side of the

Euphrates. It's the road all travelers follow from India to the west. Some men will one day call this route the Fertile Crescent.

The three magi rode into the afternoon sun; it was a huge orange wafer setting in the receding horizon before them. Jewel pointed back across the Euphrates to a weather-beaten ziggurat on the eastern horizon across the river. He explained,

"People in that area tell visitors that's the Tower of Babel. The herdsmen in the area pass on the tradition that all the people living on the earth after the flood built the pyramid as a temple to worship the sun-god of the day and the moon-god of the night. There are astrological charts at the top of that ziggurat where the original magi carved their records in stone."

"Why don't the magi go there today to study what the original magi learned?"

"Ha," Jewel explained. "The magi don't believe the tradition that God visited the construction on the pyramid. They don't believe what they haven't seen. They don't believe God confused the language of the people."

"Look," Jewel pointed. "From here you can see the flat top of the pyramid—it was never finished." He explained God stopped the people from building the pyramid by confusing everyone's language. They eventually drifted away.

"Do you believe that?" Melchior asked.

"Based on inside information, I believe that's the way it happened."

"Do you believe that this ziggurat is the actual Tower of Babel?" Melchior asked his servant. He was expecting a direct answer.

"Men don't know if this is the actual place or not." Jewel qualified his answer. Magi not only analyze answers they hear, but also they ask questions to analyze the thoughts of others. Melchior thought Jewel knew more than he spoke.

The three magi stopped to view the ruins of the ziggurat across the Euphrates. Jewel gave them another historical lesson.

"The three sons of Noah left the ark after the flood. God commanded them to go into all the world to repopulate the world. But men were disobedient. They and their children stayed here at the Euphrates and began building the tallest tower ever. It's called the Tower of Babel. Within a short time they corrupted their worship of God, worshiping the sun, moon, and stars. They worshiped what they couldn't understand."

"Then God confused their languages at the Tower of Babel—the name means 'confusion.' The children of the three sons of Noah left the Euphrates. The children of Ham went to Africa. The children of Shem, the Semitic people, settled in Asia. The children of Japheth went to Europe.

"Now here we are three magi. Each of you symbolically represents the three sons of Noah," Jewel said. Melchior was a Semitic from Persia whose lineage could be traced back to Shem. Balthazar was an African whose line extended back to Ham. Gaspar was the European magian who represented Japheth. Then Jewel added, "Each of you is representative of your people."

Then Jewel added to their thoughts,

"You are symbolizing the people of the world coming together to recognize the birth of God's Son into the world."

During the next few days, they saw the larger towns on the other side of the Euphrates River. Some of these towns still had operative ziggurats. These pyramids were where people worshiped their deity.

"There is water for the camels and food to purchase on this side of the Euphrates," Jewel explained. "If we visited the Magi in each town, we could enjoy the protection of their chantry. But we would get in endless discussions over the things we have learned. If the lead Magian learned of the Western star we saw, we would stay at each chantry two or three days explaining what we saw and defending why we are going to see the Child-King. Each Magian would waste our time, perhaps even diverting us from our pilgrimage."

The Magi agreed they would continue their journey. However, each one desired to sleep in a chantry; none of them enjoyed sleeping on the ground.

Jewel announced, "Tomorrow we'll see the city of Haran on the other side of the Euphrates. It's the city where Abraham stayed for 25 years until his father Terah died. Apparently Abraham's father would not cross into the West and leave his home in the East. When Tehran died, Abraham left Haran to go into the Promised Land."

All three magi had a sketchy idea of the story. Then Jewel explained that they would also see the city of Carchemish the next day. "That's where the first major world battle took place between the East and the West." Jewel explained how the Egyptian Pharaoh Neco left the Nile River to drive his army all the way to the Euphrates River. "Pharaoh Neco wanted to conquer all the land between these two great rivers: Nile, the river of Africa, and the Euphrates, the river of Asia."

Jewel explained how Nebuchadnezzar of Babylon defeated Pharaoh Neco at Carchemish. Egypt was never again a world power.

"You know so much of the past," Gaspar congratulated Jewel on his knowledge. But he responded,

"Every Jewish boy who learns the Scriptures knows as much."

The following day they left the Euphrates and Carchemish, heading toward Damascus, the oldest continuing city in the Near East. They did not go across the great Syrian Desert, but followed the trade route around the desert, the one that Jewel said one day would be called the Fertile Crescent. They followed the highway through the green foothills where there was water to drink and an occasional village where they could buy food to eat.

1 3

BALTHAZAR SEDUCED
WITH LUST FOR A THRONE

··

Fleshly Lust for Kingdom Power

The three magi did not reached Damascus that day; the sun was setting over the Jabal and Ruwaq Mountains, and they didn't want to enter the city after dark. They made camp in the foothill of the Al Mieha Mountains, the lowest peak in the hills. A strong eastern breeze whipped down the mountains behind them. Jewel found a protected cove between two large rocks that backed up against a shallow cave in the steep hill. They would be comfortable out of the wind.

They saw some evening camp fires outside the walls of Damascus, perhaps an hour's camel ride from the city. The three magi sat drinking tea around a warming fire. They assumed the fires in the distance were from nomadic tribes.

"Those fires represent various tribes from all across the world," Jewel began to explain. "They are like us; they do not sleep in the city. They camp outside the walls to stay with their own people."

That afternoon several groups had passed them, heading toward the city. Some of the groups included travelers on horses riding to Damascus. Jewel was concerned about one black man on horseback. He seemed overly curious about the three magi, staring intently at each; the one about whom he seemed most curious was Balthazar. They were both from Africa.

Was the stranger looking for someone he knew?

That day's trip had been tiring. They battled a howling wind through the mountains all day. But now to relax before an inviting restful sleep.

"Wheet . . . wheen . . . whooo . . . ." All three magi heard the soft enchanting tune from a flute. Out in the darkness, a solitary tune drifted into the camp and floated around the fire. The tune touched the chords of their heart. Excitement . . . love . . . romance . . . was in the air. But the tune also made the heart fearful . . . danger . . . don't come near. They didn't know the music-maker, nor did they know his intent.

All three magi sat up stiffly staring into the darkness but saw nothing. Jewel frowned because he thought the music came from the black man he saw that afternoon staring at Balthazar. He felt threatened, and that worried him.

"Play it again," Balthazar yelled into the dark.

Then turning to the other two magi, Balthazar explained, "I recognize that music; it's a bamboo reed from Ethiopia . . . ." Jewel wanted to interrupt the music. Balthazar put his finger to his lips to silence his friends. "That's a pipe from Ethiopia I heard as a child." The Ethiopian magian explained he first heard a pipe like that played by his grandfather. It put the family to sleep each night. He also remembered the pipe was played when men gathered to drink and carouse. Then with a broad laugh, he confessed, "That's the music a man plays to seduce a woman." Balthazar smiled to himself. "I haven't heard that sound since I was young."

Then Melchior almost laughed out loud. "That pipe is played by young lovers to entice one another, for the pipe touched the sensual nerves of my heart." Then they were startled by a loud voice,

"May I come into your fire?"

"Who are you?" Jewel yelled back into the darkness, reaching for a knife and slipping it into his waist band.

Walking from the darkness into the perimeter of the light was a strong muscular black body. Jewel stared intently but couldn't determine if he was the rider on the afternoon horse. His big smile disarmed the three magi, and they smiled back. Jewel didn't smile.

"My name is Selassie," the deep-voiced stranger introduced himself.

"And I am Balthazar from the tribe of the headwaters of the Nile River." Balthazar quickly explained his father was Zambia, the king of southern Ethiopia and was from a tribe of notable leaders of the government, leaders of families, and protectors of women and children.

Selassie introduced himself and told of his tribe. Balthazar didn't like what he heard. Selassie came from a clan known as liars and drunkards, a people who took advantage of the poor and weak, stealing and killing those who resisted.

"I was glad to hear about you, Balthazar," Selassie complimented his host. "You are from an outstanding tribe near the headwaters of the Nile River."

Selassie quickly changed the subject. "I am with a group of Ethiopian nomads–at least that is what people call us. We're heading back to our country in Ethiopia. We live off the land and borrow what we need. It'll take a couple of years, but we'll eventually make it back to our home in Ethiopia . . . come go with us."

Jewel poured the visitor some tea but never took his eyes off his guest. Jewel slipped one hand under his tunic on his dagger. They talked about the cold biting wind. Then, in the middle of the conversation, Selassie told Balthazar, "I have a surprise for you!" but didn't tell what it was. After more talking, Balthazar asked,

"What is your surprise?" remembering it had been promised.

"There's a young lady out in the darkness who speaks your

dialect; she's from your people. May I invite her into the warmth of the fire and into your hearts?"

All three magi looked again into the darkness, not knowing if this strange woman was the only one out there. Who else was there? Was there any danger?

Selassie put his lips to the reed to again play low notes of sensual feelings and pulsation.

Into the dim light danced a beautiful sexy body, shimmering to the low groans of the pipe, immediately capturing Balthazar's eyes. It would not be long until she captured his passion. Melchior hadn't seen an Ethiopian woman since he left home. His eyes studied her bodily features. He remembered the earrings . . . the plaits in the woman's hair, and her facial features. But his eyes returned to the voluptuous woman dancing in the sand. Her eyes stared at Balthazar's eyes, ignoring the other two magi and Jewel. The other two magi were entertained by the music, but Balthazar was addicted to the dancing woman; he couldn't take his eyes off her body. As long as the music played, he heard nothing else in the stillness of the desert night.

As she moved closer to Balthazar, she attempted to sexually entice him with suggestive dancing. Then Xeses–the woman, sister to Selassie–dramatically finished the dance by crumpling to the sand in front of Balthazar. He helped her to her feet and embraced her as a brother to a sister, or a friend to a friend, but her return was more sensual. She kissed him sensuously on the lips. Balthazar felt excitement in the pit of his stomach, but he was still naive, not realizing Xeses' intent.

"I, Balthazar, am the son of the king. I was destined to be the king of my people, but Romans captured many of us. Roman chains bound our feet. We were marched to the head waters of the Nile and placed on a flat boat into Egypt. We were sold in a Roman slave market. When a Roman makes a slave, he takes them as far from their home as possible so the slave is not tempted to run away to return home.

Balthazar was fascinated with Xeses, transfixed with the thoughts of girls he remembered from home . . . captivated by her eyes . . . hair . . . body . . . and her kiss. His thoughts about her were confusing.

Would she make a fitting queen?

Selassie saw lust in Balthazar's eyes. The fellow Ethiopian saw that Balthazar couldn't take his eyes off his sister. Balthazar was not looking at her face; his eyes wandered over her entire body. "Does she kiss everyone like that? My mother and sisters didn't kiss me like that."

"Would you like to sleep with her tonight?" Selassie asked. "She's a virgin, and I would give her to you because I know you are a man of destiny."

"No . . . no . . . no!" Jewel shouted authoritatively from the edge of the darkness. "I am a Jew who worships the Creator God. In the beginning God created man after His image, and made woman from the side of man. He gave the man and woman to each other to become one flesh, in the pledge of marriage."

Then Jewel summarized, "You must not sleep with a woman until you marry her."

"You only speak to us in platitudes," Selassie rebuked Jewel. Then Selassie turned to the other magi, "Didn't God give man an appetite to be satisfied by a woman?"

"You do not know the Hebrew Bible, nor do you know our God," Jewel blurted out his defense. "God gave us ten laws by which we live; we call them the Ten Greats, and one of them says, "Thou shall not commit adultery." Then Jewel explained the three magi were on a journey to follow a supernatural star they had seen in the Western sky. Jewel explained they were searching for the Baby-King who would be King of the Jews, and ultimately King of the Universe.

"I don't understand any of that," Selassie said, "We will talk privately in the morning," pointing to Balthazar. He assumed since they had the same skin color, they had the same appetites.

All night long, Balthazar struggled because his blanket was empty and cold. Yes, it would be good to have a warm woman's embrace for sleep. Yes, it would be good to have a woman with the same cultural roots, but his conscience gnawed at him. He had read the Psalms. He read Gasper's copy of Isaiah, and he had read a copy of the Pentateuch that belonged to Melchior. He had seen the star in the western sky and knew it was sent from God. He was searching for the star because he believed it would lead to the Baby-King who would be King of the Universe.

But Balthazar felt kindred with these new friends who were his people. They had the same skin, same facial features, and they danced to the same music. Then his stomach couldn't forget the kiss.

Balthazar wondered if this new brother could help him restore his father's kingdom. This new brother was from the other side of the lake. Could the people of this brother place him on the throne? And this new woman, Xeses—was she fit to be his queen?

Passion keeps a man from sleeping, so Balthazar did not sleep much that night. He prayed for God to help him make a decision, even prayed for God to tell him what to do. But God built choice into the heart of each human. Balthazar had to make a decision. Would it be made on the color of skin or on the star? What would he do?

That night Balthazar kept looking out from under his blanket, searching the sky for the miraculous star. But it couldn't be seen. A thick cloud covered the desert sky. No moon . . . no stars . . . no supernatural star . . . nothing. Balthazar was shut up to the image of his mind. He could see the star in his head he looked again. Heaven was still shut up with a blanket of clouds.

"Why, God, can't I see the star," then Balthazar exclaimed, "when I need it the most?"

The following morning, Jewel nudged his blanket, "You need some tea?"

"Yes," Balthazar needed some tea so his head would be as

clear as the new day. The sun was beginning to burn off any dew left over from the night.

Balthazar looked at Xeses, and she smiled back at him. In that exchange Balthazar realized that she appeared differently in the day than she did last night. It's amazing what light does to the perceptions formed in night's darkness, especially perceptions formed by erotic music. In the early morning, there was no music playing like the tune that attracted him last evening. In the daylight he saw wrinkles around her eyes . . . hard eyes. Even the mouth that gave him a smooth kiss was hard. The face showed signs of anger and deception. For the first time, he was seeing her face as it really was. Last night, he couldn't take his eyes off her body. This morning, Balthazar didn't see any of the purity he thought was there last night. Could she have existed in his mind and not in reality? He thought, *These eyes have tempted many men.* Balthazar decided to test her to see how she would respond.

"Xeses, would you greet me on this new day with a kiss of love?"

She ran over, threw her body on top of his. She provocatively kissed him; again, there was a rush to his stomach. But this time, Balthazar's body didn't respond in giddy excitement, but revulsion. He thought, *This is not a kiss of pure love; this tastes like stale wine or poison. If I drink too much of it, I will be diseased for life. Could this kiss kill?*

In many love affairs, the kiss seals the vow of the heart. But in this case, the kiss revealed the deception of the heart. A night of confusing passion became clear in the early morning sunlight.

A moment of passion will not lead to the throne. My empty blanket deceived me last night. There is no trip to Ethiopia, and there is no throne left for me.

Balthazar did not talk to Selassie; rather, he turned to his two magi friends,

"Last night, I was tempted to return to Ethiopia, the land of my birth and the people of my skin. But today, I believe the truth of the star I saw in the western sky. I know we will find the star that will lead us to the Baby-King. I expect to offer him my frankincense." Gaspar and Melchior nodded in approval.

"Let us make our way to Damascus."

Damascus is the crossroads of the nations where East meets West. The city is a mixture of the old exotic East and new modern Rome. All trade from the West funnels through Damascus going to the East and beyond.

The city is like a massive beehive, thousands of short streets where people live: blind alleys that lead nowhere, cul-de-sacs cutting off cultural communities from one another. Each one different from the one next to it. It's impossible to walk through the city from one side to the other. Yet there is one street running from the east gate to the west gate, called Straight. Both sides of the streets are lined with shops where the buyer may purchase the finest silk from India, or the best wool from the lambs of the desert. The purchaser could see Roman sandals for men, or the latest Roman fashions for the women. The merchants are crafty, taking coins from Persia or the Roman denarius. They all delight in pure gold or silver weighed out on the merchant's scales, which are never honest.

The three magi rode through the city atop their camels, navigating the street called Straight. They did not cause a great stir because the people had constantly seen long caravans wind their way through the city on the street called Straight. Also they had seen a wide variety of colorful clothing and all types of headwear. So the magi's red and green pants and three-corner hats did not attract any attention. What did catch the eye of shop owners were potential customers. They ran alongside the camels holding aloft their bargains and treasures to be sold.

Wine from Italy,
Pastel cotton from Egypt,
Turkish purple cloth, and
Shoes from Cyprus . . . .

Jewel told the three magi not to respond and never make eye contact. Even if they said, "No," that was the beginning of a conversation that never ended until the persistent shop owner made his sale. So the magi stared straight ahead. They did not stop in Damascus. They were committed to the star. No restful inns for the evening; they would camp in the hills tonight.

They headed to Eastern Syria and the double range of Jabal and Nusayriyah and Al-Ansariyah mountains.

1 4

GASPAR TEMPTED TO THE LIFE OF A KING

···

With Wealth, Could Gasper Return Home to Claim His Throne?

"*STOP!!!*" Jewel yelled loudly, interrupting the thoughts of the three magi. They looked from their camels to see a victim lying in the road being beaten by thieves, a white regal stallion standing innocently by.

"*STOP!!!* . . . Soldiers are coming . . . ." Jewel yelled an innocent threat. There were no soldiers anywhere, but it was the first thing in his mind. His strong authoritarian voice scared the robbers. They quickly looked up . . . then scooped up valuables . . . and ran into the rocks.

"Wait here." Jewel barked orders to the three magi sitting atop their camels. This was the first actual danger they had faced since leaving Persia.

"The thieves may be lurking in the rocks," Jewel cautioned.

The magi were riding the flat Jordan River road toward Jerusalem. The Holy City was only two days away, and they thought they were protected because they were in the Holy Land, a nation protected by Roman soldiers. The robbers had jumped from a large rock overhanging the roadway, knocking the victim to the ground. They beat him with clubs, caring not whether they killed their victim or not. All they wanted was his money belt, clothing, and shoes.

Jewel quickly ran to the unconscious victim. His moans told Jewel the man was not dead. Taking a water bottle, he cleansed the head wound and offered him something to drink.

"Please help me . . . I will reward you richly. . ."

Many rich think that their money can buy them anything, and when in desperate straits, they offer money for healing, even for life itself.

"I will pay you handsomely," the rich man kept repeating. "Believe me . . . ."

The three magi surrounded the victims, letting Jewel care for his physical needs.

The victim was an elderly man, as old as the three magi. He was balding with long grey stringy hair, which was now blood-matted. The finely embroidered blue silk blouse was not everyday clothing. Now it was bloody. His expensive linen tunic—torn—reflected his riches. The man had been on important business or out to dinner with friends.

"I don't live far from here," his words broke off into nothing. "I will pay you handsomely if you take me home . . . ."

Jewel wiped his face with a wet cloth. Gaspar saw that he was fair-skinned, like him. *Perhaps he's a Roman, attached to the government*, Gaspar thought to himself.

Inspecting the rich man carefully, Gaspar saw that he had a fair complexion and white legs. He was not tan-skinned as the Jews in the area, nor did he appear to be Arab or from one of the surrounding nations. Gaspar again thought, *How did he get into this area?* Later they would find out that the rich man was Flavias, a former consulate with the Roman government of Galilee. He was a courtier to King Herod; he had used his position to acquire great wealth, and with it, he began purchasing farmland in the rich flat Jordan River valley, then built a mansion. No cost was too great for his home. Whereas many of his wealthy friends used the perfect granite from the Holy Land, Flavius imported the finest white marble from the Baka Valley 100 miles away. He spared no expense to impress his friends, but everything was also his statement of his own self-identity.

Flavias wanted everyone to know he was rich and took occasions to flaunt his wealth. Opulence was reflected in his clothing; large jewels were mounted on his rings, which were now stolen. Even his spotless white stallion was a statement of wealth. It was the fastest horse around. He had even taken it to Jericho to enter into horse races.

Whenever there was danger, Flavias boasted, "I can outrun the fastest of the robbers." He didn't plan on a quick assault from a high overarching rock. He didn't plan on being knocked to the ground and beaten viciously.

"This fragrance is for healing," young Gaspar replied, pouring myrrh into the wounds. But this was no ordinary myrrh, this was some of the myrrh Gaspar had reserved to present to the Baby-King. When the cask was opened, the fragrance enveloped the roadside. The smell invigorated Flavias as well as the three magi and Jewel himself. The life-giving fragrance gave hope to Flavias. And without anyone realizing, the myrrh invigorated them all.

"Ohhhhhhh." Jewel couldn't tell whether it was a moan of enjoyment or a moan of pain. Some healing medicines had to sting before they energized, and the myrrh was no different. Brushing on myrrh cleans the dirt out of wounds; the stinging pain means health. Flavias would be better . . . he would live.

"I will pay for the myrrh," Flavius offered.

Gaspar placed Flavias on his own camel and walked beside him to make sure he didn't fall. The myrrh had done its intended task; Flavias ached all over but with full consciousness, was able to balance himself to sway gently to the gait of the camel.

Gaspar could barely make out the distant huge white building in the evening gloaming. The servants had lit torches in the courtyards and on both sides of the front gate to welcome their master home.

When they arrived at the massive gate, the attendant quickly alerted other servants who swarmed into action around Gaspar's camel. Flavias was still weak, and four servants, one on each end of a blanket, carried him gently but quickly to his bedroom.

Flavias barked orders,

"Put my friends in the best bedrooms for tonight. Each shall have his private room . . . and a private room for the servant, Jewel."

The spotless white marbled halls gave evidence of continual care. There were burning olive oil lamps, and torches were lit in each of the guest rooms.

Gaspar was shown to the largest bedroom of all; the servants placed small lamps around the room to illuminate its features.

This is a room fit for a king, Gaspar thought to himself. *If I were king, I would sleep in a room like this every night.*

Gaspar thought back to his first glimpse of the gleaming white marble palace. *The most luxurious home I've seen since I left Tarsus*, Gaspar again thought. This was the palace of the king.

Gaspar had seen how carefully and tenderly the servants took care of their master, as though each one wanted to do more than the other. And their service was not out of fear; there was respect and love in their eyes. As Gaspar went to sleep, he thought to himself,

"Hmm . . . *I wonder what it would be like to live in splendor like this?*

When Gaspar awakened the next morning, he was surprised to see a large bronze bathtub in the corner of the room. The servants filled it with warm water, so quietly he did not know they had even entered the room. Neatly folded towels and slippers awaited him.

As he sank into the warm suds, Gaspar planned to stay there until the water turned cold. *This is how I would live when I become king.* He let his thoughts drift into what might have been had it not been for the treachery of his brothers. His thoughts were interrupted by a servant bringing him a cup of hot tea,

"Jewel sends hot tea for your morning wake." The tea was enjoyable, but it was not the same without Jewel serving it.

During the morning, Gaspar walked the grounds, talking to the various servants. There were many shepherds keeping sheep for Flavias, over 10,000 in his herd. There were milk cows for fresh milk, and chickens for eggs, and each day an animal was butchered and roasted—meat for all servants and guests.

In a small white building not far away was a bakery. The smell of fresh baked bread tempted Gaspar. It was prepared daily for Flavias and everyone else.

There were stables for horses and cows, and barns for grain grown in the fields. Because of the rich harvest, Flavias had added a new barn each year, just to hold the increase.

"**COME** . . . . You must come immediately! The master wants to see you," one of the tan-skinned servants summoned Gaspar to see Flavius. The servant didn't say why, nor did he give any explanation other than, "**COME**."

Gaspar didn't know, but the stablemen had been directed by Flavius to postpone the journey of the three magi. The stablemen gave excuses for not preparing their camels. "We must rest the camels; we know what camels need . . . We have washed your blankets and they are wet . . . and the harnesses on the animals are worn out and we must replace them." Melchior and Balthazar sat on the upper porch, discussing reasons why they were being delayed.

"Flavius is a politician and he has his reasons," suggested Melchior.

"I don't trust him or any politician," responded Balthazar.

Flavius was sitting up in his bed when Gaspar entered the room. Bandages were on his head wounds. After greeting Gaspar, he downplayed his injuries. "They're nothing . . . they will be much better in a day or two."

Then Flavius got immediately to the point, "You spoke to me in two or three languages that I didn't understand . . . then you spoke in Latin and the language of Tarsish. I understood them." Flavius only spoke Latin and Armenian, and he recognized the language of Tarsish and Spain.

"I knew you were civilized and would not harm me."

Gaspar responded politely, indicating he would have come to help whether he was a slave or a rich man.

"I felt your compassion as you cleansed my wounds with myrrh. This is a rich ointment that you sacrificed for me."

"I would have done it for anyone," Gaspar replied.

Flavius thanked Gaspar several times, offering to pay him for the myrrh.

"No," Gaspar suggested. "Giving gifts, whether expensive or not, is who I am," Gaspar replied. "I live with an open hand to others and an open hand to God."

"When you sat me on your own camel, I recognized that as an act of brotherhood and deep compassion." Flavius explained that men do not offer their camel to others, nor do they ride anyone but family and close friends.

"But you were hurt badly."

Flavius expressed lengthy appreciation, recalling all the things that Gaspar had done for him. Then he noted,

"Your Latin was learned in Italy or Spain; it is the pure form of speech given by the gods." Then he went on to ask, "Who are you, and where did you come from?"

Gaspar told the whole story of growing up in the regions of Spain—Tarsish—being the firstborn son of a king and heir to the throne in their small city-state. He told of being sold as a slave . . . put on a ship bound for Antioch. Flavius asked many questions about the role of the king, and Gaspar answered them all to his satisfaction. Flavius nodded in approval to each answer.

"I want you to come live with me . . . . I want you to leave your excursion to find the star and the Baby-King." Flavius explained that Gaspar was already in the Holy Land, and that he could do more for Gaspar than any king might do for him in the future. Then Flavius noted,

"After all, you're not a king; you don't need to bring a gift to this Baby-King. You're only in the line to the monarchy."

Flavius then tried to persuade Gaspar, "Look at my estate, the servants, the cattle and livestock, a house much too large for me . . . everything will be at your disposal."

Why . . .? thought Gaspar. Then he repeated his question out loud, "Why are you offering me all this?"

"Because your spirit is as my spirit. We have a similar heritage . . . similar culture . . . and similar language." He went on to explain, "Each evening I would enjoy having conversations with you after the evening meal. Then as I attend political functions for King Herod, I would like you to go with me. Your royal upbringing would go well for me."

"Let me think about it for a little while." Gaspar immediately began to run thoughts through his mind. *I would have all the money I would ever need for the rest of my life . . . servants to wait on me . . . government to protect me . . . and enough money to travel . . .*

The thought of travel burst on his mind like a supernova. He could book passage back to Spain, visit his home country, even perhaps have an opportunity to regain the throne. Gaspar realized this was a great opportunity. Almost unlimited wealth and unlimited opportunities.

Then Gaspar said to Flavius, "I must tell my friends to ask their opinion."

"BONG . . . BONG . . . BONG." The sound of a deep-ringing bell filled the room. "Lunch is ready," Flavius announced.

During lunch, Gaspar had difficulty eating. He wanted to talk with his two friends about the offer of wealth, but he couldn't discuss it freely in front of Flavius. So he said nothing. Embarrassment kept him silent. The tension between blurting out the offering yet reservedly explaining it to friends overwhelmed him.

After lunch, the three magi sat alone on the upper porch. A warm breeze from the desert drifted up the Jordan River valley from Jericho. The two friends listened carefully as Gaspar explained the offer that was made to him.

Balthazar spoke first, "Happiness is an elusive pursuit in life. More than one pair of shoes does not make you happy; only having comfortable shoes satisfies you. And having two camels does not make you more important; it's the camel on which you are riding that's important. And having two roasted glazed ducks does not satisfy the appetite; only one in your mouth will satisfy." Gaspar heard the hyperbole and waited to see if Balthazar would interpret it. It wasn't long before the Ethiopian magian suggested,

"If a long journey to find the King of the World will make you happy, think of what happens when you actually find Him. Will worshiping the Baby-King bring the greatest happiness in life?"

The atmosphere on the porch grew silent. "So, I must complete my journey to find happiness?" Gaspar asked a question that would not be answered.

Melchior had been listening intently to the wisdom of his Ethiopian friend. Then he waited for a lull in the conversation to suggest,

"How many rich men do you know that have real pleasure in life? They constantly worry about losing their riches, and so they never enjoy the riches they have. And no matter how much a rich man has, he is usually not completely happy. How much will make a rich man happy, a little more?"

Melchior got up from his chair and walked over to the railing. The elderly magian invited the younger Gaspar, "Look out on this vast estate. We see trees with all types of fruit, we see fields growing grain, and we see servants everywhere. Will this make you happy? Or will you need a larger estate and a house made of ivory, silver, and gold? If you seek happiness and pleasure in the material things of this life, what will happen when they cannot give pleasure?"

Early the next morning before the sun came up, Jewel led the three magi and their camels down the long lane leading to the Jordan River road. They had said goodbye to Flavius the night before. Gaspar had told him that he would be on his journey and that his life would not be happy until he had worshiped the Baby-King who would one day rule the world. As they turned right on the Roman road, the sun peeked up over the Wadi Rum Mountains of Ammon.

1 5

ARRIVING IN JERUSALEM
....

The Beginning of the End

The camels of the magi were slowly trudging up the path of a steep, narrow valley that led to the top of mountains where Jerusalem is located. The magi didn't know it at the time, but the narrow pass through the mountain rocks was a high crime area. It would eventually be known as "the valley of the shadow of death" because thieves lurked there.

The inn halfway up the valley trail on the right side of the road would later be called The Inn of the Good Samaritan. They stopped for water and to stretch their legs but continued climbing on their surefooted camels; they were anxious to get to Jerusalem.

"It's not very far," Jewel shouted back to the magi. He didn't tell them, but he had seen the holy city many times from many vantage points. But this time, Jewel was excited and his legs were light, and his feet pumped steadily. *I must see Herod's temple, named after Herod the Great. People say it's the most magnificent house of worship in the world.*

Jewel was Jewish–the magi thought–but even then, the magi wouldn't understand the words that faithful Hebrews sang when they climbed the ascents to the temple.

> *How lovely is your dwelling place,*
> *O LORD of Heaven's Armies.*

I long, yes, I faint with longing
to enter the courts of the LORD.
With my whole being, body, and soul,
I will shout joyfully to the living God.
When I enter her gates.
(Psalms 84:1-2)

Once more, Jewel yearned to experience the presence of God in the temple. He continued singing,
Even the sparrow finds a home there
and the swallow builds her nest
and raises her young—
at a place near your altar.
(Psalm 84:3)

Three times a year, every Jewish male was required to come to Jerusalem to seek the presence of God. As they made the long trek up the valley, they realized robbers and muggers hid in the rocks looking for victims. That's why the valley is called the Shadow of Death.

Right before cresting the final hill, Jewel brook into song.
Open for me the gates where the righteous enter,
and I will go in and thank the LORD.
Those gates lead to the presence of the LORD,
and the godly enter there
(Ps. 118:19-20).

Then suddenly, Jewel was at the top of the hill, and he saw the east gate into the temple sparkling like gold in the rising sun. He fell to his knees and again broke into song.

This is the day the LORD has made,
We will rejoice and be glad in it.
Please, Lord, please save us.

Please, Lord, please give us success.
Bless the one who comes in the name of the Lord.
We bless You from the house of the Lord
(Ps. 118:24-26).

The three magi stood on the top of the hill in disbelief . . . speechless! Herod's Temple was more magnificent than they expected. No thoughts came to their minds . . . no response . . . they were emotionally captured by the magnificence of Herod's Temple.

The morning sun bounced golden rays off of its sparkling walls, making the temple itself appear to be gold. But not gold in value but precious in brilliance . . . like gold that excites the consumer . . . like gold that demands rapt attention . . . like gold that stirs greed and passion.

Each of the magi had read descriptions in scrolls and charts that captured their imagination, but Herod's Temple did more than capture; it enslaved them.

The magi knew that they could not enter Jerusalem through the temple for they were not circumcised, that is, except Jewel. He was Jewish. So they spotted the gate to the temple's immediate right. The Sheep Gate. The gate was high, so they didn't need to disembark from their camels. The official caravans representing foreign governments entered other gates.

The small caravan of three magi on Persian camels attracted little attention. No one stopped to stare. They had seen caravans enter their city on many occasions from all points east. That included east of Persia, from India itself. Their bright green pants drew attention mostly from curious children who had never seen them before. People of Jerusalem wore white tunics, and Jerusalem dress blended everyone together.

The Persian magi wore shoes with the toes pointed upward, whereas feet in Jerusalem were shod with sandals.

People on a compelling journey usually don't identify why

they're traveling. The magi sat erect on their camels as if to say "Don't ask me anything." Their speech reflected the intent of their journey.

Shepherds were leading their herds into the city to sell sheep to the city dwellers. Right inside the Sheep Gate was a large open area where various herds were waiting to be sold.

Looking around, they saw animal waste; that was no place for the magi to stop and rest. Jewel motioned for them to follow him,

"I know the perfect place to rest . . . ."

Near the Sheep Gate, they found the pool of Bethesda, a deep cistern in the ground that holds water for the city. Surrounding the pool of Bethesda are many shops and outdoor places to eat and drink. There were also a few palm trees that offered shade from the seat; otherwise, tables and chairs were placed in the shade near to buildings.

The camel driver banged the knees of each camel, making it kneel. The magi never forgot that they were magi, but in their kingly self-perception, they desired to be considered monarchs. So they held themselves regally as a king would do when alighting from his camel.

People were milling around, some going and coming from the temple approximately a block away. There were several courtyards with tables for relaxing and eating. The three wise men saw a table in a secluded courtyard where they could be alone. Melchior, the oldest—also the self-proclaimed leader—was the first to descend from his camel, and he walked as in procession over to the table to be seated. The others followed in like manner.

Jewel scurried to a small, smoking fire without flames. Blowing on the coals, they slowly turned red, and then finally a small yellow flame trickled out of the few pieces of charcoals left. Before long, Jewel's custom teapot was singing a tune to notify all that tea was ready.

Then some curious elderly men secured enough

confidence to come take a small table next to the magi. They were surprised that the magi spoke in Hebrew. However, although the dialect was different, still they could communicate.

"I brought the tea from Persia." Jewel's words broke the silence. Then to make sure the men from Jerusalem appreciated his efforts, the old servant added, "There's no tea in the Holy Land."

That interaction allowed the elderly men to ask the magi about their journey, and especially about the Euphrates River. The river always intrigued the city dwellers of Jerusalem. Finally, the key question came up.

"Why are you in Jerusalem?"

It seemed a harmless question, yet the answer would tell the Jerusalemites much about these travelers. It would tell them why they'd come so far. There had to be a compelling reason to travel over 1000 miles to visit Jerusalem. One of them wanted to know,

"Are you here to worship in the temple . . .?"

"Have you come on official business for your country . . .?"

"Have you come to see Herod the Great . . .?"

"Are you here to bring sacrifices in the temple and worship Jehovah?"

Melchior looked from one set of magian eyes to the other, not knowing how to answer the question . . . or when to say it. They all had a mission, and each was reluctant to tell what he knew. Each magian waited for the other. Then, Melchior, the oldest, stroked his long, gray beard. The men from Jerusalem knew that Melchior had something important to say. Then Melchior slowly spoke,

"We have seen a spectacular star in your western sky. We know the supernatural star announced the coming of the Jewish-Deliver. We also have studied your Scripture and know He will be born to a virgin. He will be a Baby-King, so we have brought Him gifts."

The three magi exchanged glances, then nodded their agreement with Melchior. They stared back at the Jerusalemites. Being uncomfortable, the city men exchanged glances among themselves. Then finally, the Jewish listener who seemed to be the oldest stroked his beard and began to ask a question,

"Is . . .?"

But Melchior cut him off deliberately.

"We know that written in the book of Moses, 'there shall come a star out of Jacob and a scepter shall arise out of Israel.'"

Then Melchior waited and said,

"We think we saw the star when we were in the East." Gaspar interrupted, "It was His star." Melchior waited for his words to sink in. Then replied, "The star was like no other star we've ever seen, and we had never seen that star before that time. We saw the star on the 25th day of the 12th month when the three stars—known as the three kings—perfectly lined up with Orion."

"What did the star look like? How do you know it was Messiah's star?"

Melchior calmly explained that they were magi from Persia. "Many magi in our country devote their lives to studying the stars. We know stars move at night from the eastern skies to the western skies, but this special star went the opposite way. We saw this magnificent star arise in the western sky. We were in Persia when we saw the star. Then it began moving the opposite way of the other stars. It began moving toward us in the west."

"Tell us more . . . ."

"His star was the brightest star we've ever seen, and it was not high in the sky as the other stars. It was low and moving."

"Hmmm . . . ."

"What could we do but follow His star . . . ?"

Then, Melchior looked at his two magi friends, not knowing what to say. He didn't want to say too much, but he could say too little. He wanted to tell them enough to get the answers he sought. He wanted to find out where the baby–called

Messiah—was born. The magi looked from one set of eyes to the other. Then Melchior asked,

"Where could we find your king? Where could we find this Baby-King?"

The Jewish men from Jerusalem were dazed by the question. Yes, every faithful Jew was looking for Messiah. Now the fearful eyes of the elderly men nervously glanced from one another. They all knew the same thing. Herod was king and was not the Messiah. Herod held the scepter, but any who challenged his rule was put to death. They all knew that Herod was cruel . . . vindictive . . . mean . . . and dangerous.

Their suspicious eyes looked at one another; their eyes nodded in silence. They knew it was dangerous to criticize Herod. Any condemning conversation could mean death. Finally, the oldest Jewish listener said,

"We have but one king . . . that is Herod the Great . . . You will find him in his palace."

The three magi exchanged knowing looks. They knew Messiah was to be born of a virgin and that He would usher in a great period of peace. Could they be looking for a son of Herod? Could Messiah be born of a virgin daughter of Herod? The magi too had heard rumors about the viciousness of Herod the Great.

The three magi did not tell of the rumored atrocities they heard. The Jewish men from the city also said nothing about the cruelty of King Herod. They agreed to keep silent, not because they had come to an agreement, but it was through eyes of fear.

The elderly city Jews each scurried his own way spreading the word that the magi in Jerusalem were looking for the child Messiah that had been born. The Jews knew that Messiah would come from the tribe of Judah, and they also knew He would usher in a time of great prosperity. They knew that Jerusalem would become the center of the earth. Deep in the heart of every Jew was the hope that Messiah would drive the Romans into the sea. The Jews hated their captors and spit on the ground behind the

Roman soldiers, careful not to be seen lest they be punished. For almost 600 years, the Jews had not controlled their city in peace. It had been almost a thousand years since David sat on the throne. Word spread throughout Jerusalem of the magi looking for the place where Messiah is born. Many asked, "Is there a new son of David who will finally sit on the throne? Will he finally exercise dominion over all of the Gentiles?"

16

CONFRONTATION IN JERUSALEM

....

Finding an Evil King

Word reached Herod the Great that three magi were in Jerusalem looking for a new born Child-King, who would be the son of David . . . who would sit upon the throne of Israel. This Child would be the King of the Jews.

Herod snarled, "I'm the King of the Jews!" His first reaction was to arrest the three magi, drag them into his courts. Then execute them. That way, he could stop any insurrection. "No child will be a threat to my throne!"

But wait! Herod thought to himself. *I can use these three magi to help me find the baby.* Herod reasoned that if the three magi would lead him to the baby. *Yes, the baby is the one I want to execute.* The three magi were no threat to his throne: it was the baby who could incite loyalty in the hearts of Jewish people, the baby who could inflame the passion of Jews to rebel against Rome and him in the backlash.

No, it's not the wise men that I want to execute. It's the baby I want to kill. Herod thought to himself.

Herod pondered whether he should search out the wise men or let them come to him. After all, he was the supreme authority. Everyone in Jerusalem needed his authority to do anything official. "No," Herod decided. "I'll let the magi come to me."

It wasn't long before a request came from the attending Roman soldiers that magi from Persia wanted an audience with Herod.

Herod decided not to let the magi know of his concern, nor would he see them immediately. He instructed the soldier to tell the magi to return the next morning, three hours after sun up. He would make room in his calendar to see them at that time.

The magi slept at an inn that night, an inn for Gentiles. A good conscientious Jew would not invite a Gentile into his home, and the magi knew this about Jewish tradition. They also knew that many of the inns in Jerusalem only took in fellow Jews. They searched the city looking for tell-tale evidences that an inn was hospitable to non-Jews. If there were Scriptures tacked to the doorframe, they would seek lodging.

That night, the three wise men planned their strategy for the following day,

"What shall we say to Herod when we meet him?" Melchior asked the question.

Balthazar suggested, "We should speak to him in Hebrew; then he'll know we understand Jewish customs. He should know we are here on a Jewish matter."

Gaspar agreed, suggesting they greet Herod the Great with Jewish greetings, rather than a Persian greeting.

"Agreed."

The following morning, the three magi found their way to Herod's palace much earlier than instructed. They were ushered into a waiting room, speaking to the Roman guards in Latin. But there was little conversation between them; someone might be listening. The magi were all business. They came to see Herod. The same with the Romans; they were all business, there to guard Herod.

"Herod is finishing his breakfast," one of the Roman officials came out of the throne room to announce.

The three magi were ushered into a high-ceilinged throne

room . . . gold walls, shining marble columns, and white glistening floors. The magi were struck with the ostentatious display of wealth and power. Peacocks walked in from the balcony door; a striped tiger chained to the wall, peered at them.

Servants scurried around the throne room, not giving much attention to the magi, but they stole glances at their clothes. The bright colors were in stark contrast to the white simplicity of Roman tunics. Roman hard leather sandals scraped on the marble floor, while the satin slippers with upturned toes tread silently, without making a sound.

The room was silent . . . waiting.

"Ding." A sound of a small bell reached every corner of the room.

Everyone stopped, frozen in their tracks. The magi felt the closeness of silence, but they also felt the presence of fear. The servants knew what the bell meant. Herod would soon make his entrance. No one must talk, no eyes looked around the room. Every eye focused on the ground until Herod made his grand entrance. A page stepped to the door and then in a loud bombastic voice announced,

"HEROD THE GREAT . . . KING OF THE JEWS . . . ."

All eyes that were looking down quickly looked up to see Herod the Great entering the room. Cheers went up from all of his admirers, followed by spontaneous applause.

The three magi looked at each other, not knowing if they should cheer. However, they did join in clapping but only with reserved dignity. Gaspar whispered under his breath to his two friends, "Should we bow in respect for Herod and his office . . . or are we kings?" The two friends did not answer the question. The emotional pressure of the moment answered for them. When Herod came face to face with the magi, all three bowed in reverence.

Looking up, Gaspar almost laughed but choked down his startled response. There, on Herod's clothes, were the crumbs and grease from breakfast. At first, Gaspar wanted to say something, but he knew better. The neurotic Herod had banished others for a lesser crime than mockery. He stifled his smile and bowed more deeply to hide his face. Gaspar smelled an odor,

Does not Herod know that a king must never appear less than perfect? His clothes must never be wrinkled, soiled, or give off a distasteful odor?

Herod mounted the stairs to his lofty throne. No one in the room was permitted to raise a head higher than Herod. When looking at him, all of his subjects did not look him in the eye but glanced downwards. They treated him with divine-like qualities. However, the Roman soldiers did not respond as the servants. They were respectful but functional in their duties.

"Why did you come to my kingdom?" Herod scowled at the magi. They sat in lower chairs, off to the left of Herod . . . where Gentiles sat. The right of Herod was reserved for Jewish dignitaries.

Melchior looked down. He knew it was his duty to answer. So he stroked his beard slowly and continually, signaling to Herod that he was preparing an answer.

This was not the Jewish hospitality they expected. Melchior thought Herod would be gracious and say, "Welcome to my kingdom . . . ." Balthazar expected Herod to greet him the way Solomon had greeted the Queen of Sheba, "May the LORD bless you and keep you, may the LORD make His face to shine upon you and give you peace . . . ." But no, Herod was a down-to-business type of king. He cared for none of the formality of greeting visitors from another land.

Gaspar was not surprised by Herod's greetings. Herod had been influenced by the Romans, and they too were a down-to-business type of people.

Again, Herod repeated his request, "Why have you come to Jerusalem?"

The question was not idle. The rumors spreading around

the city had gotten Herod's attention. He knew that the magi had been asking throughout the city where the Christ Child was born, King of the Jews.

Herod was not in a mood to be nice to the magi. He wanted to bring this conversation to a swift end.

Melchior, the spokesman for the magi, waited until Herod seemed to cool down. Then he raised one hand slightly to capture Herod's attention. Melchior decided he would not greet Herod in peace, nor would he wish blessings upon him. Melchior asked, "Where is the newborn King of the Jews born?" Then he went on to add, "When we were in the East, we saw His star in the western sky over Jerusalem, and we have come to worship Him."

There, the gauntlet was on the table. The magi had heard that Herod was neurotic and vicious. He killed usurpers to his throne. Melchior decided not to play games with Herod but to tell him plainly why they had come to Jerusalem.

Now, the issue was clearly open. The issue was the baby who was born King of the Jews. The magi wanted to know how Herod would handle this issue.

The magi thought that perhaps the baby had been born to Herod's family. Since the baby was young and Herod was old, perhaps Herod would want his progeny to sit on his throne. Herod must know that he could not live long enough to keep the baby from the throne. The magi thought that perhaps the baby would be a son or grandson of Herod.

Herod was disturbed by the quick clear answer. He began to calculate the time when they saw the star, stating, "So you saw the star approximately a year ago on the seventh month in the Jewish calendar?"

The answer began to change Herod's mood. Rather than alienate the magi or threaten them, he decided to get all the information from them possible.

Hmmm . . . Herod again thought to himself. *That means the child must be around one year old.*

Now Herod had more information. He knew the exact time when the star had appeared; now he had to find the exact location. Again, Herod thought to himself, *I must humor these magi and make them like me.*

Clapping his hands out loud, he summoned the attention of all the people in the page room.

"**QUICK** . . ., go find the religious scholars and bring them to me . . . **NOW**."

The room sprang into action. Herod returned his glance to the magi and said, "I do not know where this child—King—will be born, but the scholars who know the Scriptures will tell us. We must wait for them to study and let us know."

Then Herod nodded his head for the magi to leave. He explained that when the Jewish scholars determined an answer, he would call for the magi.

"Tomorrow . . . tomorrow, we will have an answer for you . . . and you can worship the Child-King."

Knowing they were dismissed, the magi turned to leave. Each obeying instinctively, not looking at the other. They had come, asked their question, and now the answer was to be found among the religious scholars.

That afternoon, Herod met with the religious scholars who were priests and teachers of the law. He was not in the mood for pleasantries or banter. Herod wanted to get right to the business at hand.

"Where do the prophets say that the child Messiah will be born?"

None of the scholars wanted to answer Herod, afraid of offending him. If one answered wrong, or they argued among themselves, Herod may execute the lot of them. So the scholars were quite aware of their precarious position.

Before coming in the room, they agreed that Levi, a priest scholar, would answer Herod's questions. Josephus, the historian who knew the geography of the land, would verify the answers for Herod. Otherwise no one else would speak, unless spoken to by Herod. That afternoon, the Jewish scholars were unusually reserved.

"In Bethlehem." Levi spoke up strongly and without hesitation. "The child is to be the Son of David, and David's city was Bethlehem." Levi went on to explain that just as David had been born in Bethlehem, the strategic city of the tribe of Judah, it was only natural that the Messiah Redeemer would be born there.

"May I quote the Scriptures to you?" Levi asked.

"Go ahead."

Levi read in Hebrew, "O Bethlehem of Judah, you are not just a lowly village of Judah, for a ruler will come out of you who shall be governor of Israel. He shall rule my people, Israel."

So Bethlehem is where the child was born." Herod thought to himself, *Bethlehem is not that big of a town. There are probably only a handful of babies.*

Herod had his answers, so he dismissed the Jewish scholars with a flick of the wrist. There was no appreciation for their coming; there was no gratitude for their answer. It was simply a flick of the wrist. Herod wanted to be rid of these pesky fanatics.

After the religious scholars had left the room, Herod turned to his page and said, "Go tell the magi that I want to see them in the morning immediately after breakfast."

It seemed that many of the faithful Jewish knew that the Messiah was to be born in Bethlehem. They knew the prophecy of Micah, and they knew that Messiah was to be the Son of David and would sit on the throne of David. They all knew that Bethlehem was David's hometown. But the magi didn't know this. They did not know about Micah's prophecy. So how could the magi know the child would be born in Bethlehem?

The following morning, they waited in the outer alcove to be summoned into Herod's throne room. Melchior warned, "Remember, gentlemen . . . we are not subject to this man, but we are guests in his kingdom." Then he explained, "Herod has great power, but his power comes from Rome. Herod is only a puppet that carries out the will of Rome. He will not humiliate us, nor will he harm us; Herod speaks for Rome who is at peace with Persia. We will be safe."

The Other Side Of The Palace

King Herod angrily stomped through the hallway of the great reception area; his red face, clenched teeth, and menacing walk told everyone, "Look out!" The word spread quickly through the palace. "Hide." And, "Don't look him in the face, look the other way."

Ten Roman soldiers dressed in battle gear waited for him at the large processional doorway. They knew something was wrong, but they didn't know what they were to do. They waited for orders.

"Don't come into the room until I call you, and when I clap my hands three times, charge into the room and arrest all three magi." Herod was afraid they may be plotting an insurrection against his throne. There were terrorists all throughout the land who would do anything for a chance to assassinate Herod . . . zealots. Then Herod spit the words out, "Zealots"; those were the ones trying to kill him.

As Herod turned toward the massive doors, instantly his anger turned into a politician's smile, like a person suffering from a bipolar disorder.

"AND NOW, KING HEROD THE GREAT, APPOINTED BY THE ROMAN SENATE, KING OF ALL JUDEA, JERUSALEM AND INTERMIA."

Herod strode cheerfully—like a politician seeking votes—into the room to greet the three magi like they were long lost friends.

"I'll not sit on the throne today." Herod spoke in a

condescending tone. "Let's sit in these chairs where we can talk about your journey . . . I'm so interested in your journey."

Gaspar again noticed the crumbs on Herod's clothes, the same that he wore yesterday. The strong body odor endured. *This is strange for a man of such great arrogance.*

Herod spoke first, repeating their question, "You asked where is the baby that is born King of the Jews." A scowl crossed his forehead as he repeated the question. But just as quickly, Herod contained himself, saying, "How long ago did you see this star—the one you call His star—in the western sky?" Herod wanted as much information from the magi as possible.

They responded, "Approximately a year ago."

This time, Herod spoke warmly. He welcomed them into his kingdom and hoped they found comfortable lodging. And Herod even hypocritically added, "I pray Jehovah God will guide your journey to find the Babe." Herod tried to convince everyone in the room of his sincerity. Herod showed great respect for the Jewish Scriptures. "They teach that God will send a Jewish leader to deliver His people and He would be born in Bethlehem." Herod said it loud enough so that everyone in the room—not only the magi–but Roman soldiers and his palace attendants heard his explanation. "This is a wonderful day that the Lord has brought to us!"

Herod explained the baby was born in Bethlehem, only a few miles away. He then added, "But we don't know the location in Bethlehem. It's a small town; you'll easily find the babe."

After the magi left Herod's court, he called over his most trusted palace guard–not a Roman solder but a Levite who followed the Sadducee tradition.

"Follow them," Herod told his trusted guard. "Don't let them out of your sight, and when you find the location of the Child who is born in Bethlehem, come to me immediately."

The palace guard pounded his fist to his chest in salute and sneered agreement with Herod,

"Yes, we will find this pretender to your throne."

Around the evening meal, the magi discussed their feelings about Herod. They genuinely liked the man and were surprised at his winsome nature and his attempt to convince them that he would truly worship the Child-King. Melchior stroked his goatee, a sign that he was in deep thought. *I think that Herod is wise enough to deceive us.* Then he spoke out loud, "Herod is probably the wisest politician we've met in a long time. He tried to convince everyone in the room that he wanted to go worship the Baby-King."

The two magi friends shook their heads in approval. "Could we outfox the fox?" Melchior asked if the star itself would help them know what to do. They left the fire and looked for their blankets; they were not rolled out for the evening the way Jewel usually prepared them. Gaspar went outdoors then a few minutes later rushed into the room, yelling, "I just saw the star again . . . it's up there . . . His star . . . it's beginning to move."

The magi immediately sprang into action. Melchior yelled, "JEWEL . . . JEWEL . . . WHERE ARE YOU?"

"The camels are ready." Jewel entered the room. "I've already loaded your gifts for the baby who is Messiah King; we must quickly follow the star . . . ." Then Jewel added, "We must go tonight so no one follows us."

"How did you know?" Melchior asked. "I just knew," was all Jewel answered as the three began to mount their camels.

"Look, the star is closer than ever before," the emotional Balthazar yelled to his friend. The star was no longer high in the sky but was so close, Balthazar felt he could reach out and touch it. As soon as they mounted their camels, the star began moving . . . south . . . slowly.

Melchior said to his friends, "The star seems to know how fast our camels can travel. It never outruns us."

"Nor does His star lag behind," Gaspar added.

THREE KINGS WORSHIP THE BABY-KING

Giving What is Most Meaningful

The finely crafted furniture in the home reflected a certain pride of ownership. Joseph had helped build furniture for many of the residents back in Nazareth. But Joseph's best work was done in Bethlehem for his wife and son. They had been in the house for a long time and planned to settle down here in their new home—forever.

"This house will do for a while," Joseph said, not looking up from his work.

The gossipers spread the lie. They suggested Joseph and Mary had sex before the marriage ceremony—and she got pregnant. So they had to get married. Some of the busybodies in Nazareth did more than think about it. They made it their business to tell everyone.

Mary and Joseph had chosen not to return to their hometown of Nazareth because the ugly rumors there made them uncomfortable. The people of Nazareth had refused to believe the talk of angelic visitations or miraculous conceptions in their midst.

"The day of miracle births has passed," the people said.

So Joseph and Mary remained in Bethlehem, the birthplace of their son. "We'll be close to the temple for the baby,"

Joseph had reasoned. "If Jesus is to be the spiritual leader of our nation, he should live near the City of God."

"But what will we do in Bethlehem?" Mary had learned something of the practical necessities of life under the tutelage of her cousin Elizabeth.

"I'll find work in a carpenter shop," Joseph insisted. "Bethlehem will be our new home."

Mary had to admit she loved their small but cozy first home. It was simply one large room, with one front door and a smaller back entrance. Because the "house room" was attached on both sides to other houses, there were no side windows. On this day, Mary had opened both doors to allow the cool morning air to ventilate the house as she cleaned up after their morning meal. Joseph sat on a stool in the corner, hand carving intricate designs on a table leg for one of his more discriminating customers. The sun was barely above the horizon.

"**Look** . . . camels are coming!!" a small boy yelled outside their door.

The streets of Bethlehem were only just awakening to morning activity, but some untold excitement had roused the neighbors from their homes. The young boy, Melki, the unofficial town crier, ran door to door yelling, *"Come see the caravan!"*

Mary gathered Jesus in her arms, and she and Joseph stepped into the street, blinking against the hazy morning sunlight as they looked toward the east end of Bethlehem. There, a large crowd of villagers gathered about the camels. Caravans stopped in Bethlehem all the time, but this was no ordinary caravan. Camels with two humps like these were seldom seen in Judea.

Jewel, driving the lead camel, was talking to Melki, the young man with the loud voice. The local youth lifted his arm and pointed a finger toward Joseph. Above the crowd of villagers, three men satastride the camels, sporting strangely colored turbans. Now all eyes were staring at Joseph down the narrow street lined with small houses. Everyone stared at Joseph and Mary—and the baby.

Melchior in his rich, gold turban whispered hurriedly to the servant Jewel in a bright green cape and brown trousers. They both turned their necks to see Joseph. The gold turban motioned, and Jewel ran towards Joseph.

Not knowing if there might be danger, Joseph spoke quietly to Mary. "Go in the house," he said. She gathered young Jesus to her breast and obeyed, but she had not gotten in the house before Jewel saw what he most wanted to see. Jewel saw the glory of God folded into the arms of His virgin mother.

In that fleeting glance, Jewel saw the Christ-Child. He looked like a normal baby, but Jewel knew better. He beheld His glory; it was the glory of the only begotten, as manifested in human flesh.

Jewel bowed to Joseph in greeting. "They tell us you are the father of a young child," he spoke in perfect Hebrew.

Joseph nodded, "Yes."

"We are searching for the One born King of the Jews."

At the phrase "King of the Jews," Joseph was startled. The angel Gabriel had told Mary that Jesus would indeed sit on the throne of David, but they hadn't dared breathe a word to anyone that Jesus would be a King. *How do they know?* Joseph thought before answering. *What do they know?*

Sensing Joseph's apprehension, Jewel again bowed deeply. His milky brown skin was smooth, and the cotton and silk in his cape beautifully woven together, not like the coarse cloth found around Bethlehem. Joseph recognized the curled toes on the man's shoes as a Persian fashion. Everyone in Palestine wore sandals.

"May we visit the young king this evening?" Jewel asked. "We have gifts for the king." Jewel turned and motioned to the three magi sitting on their camels. "The gifts are from the three magi."

Joseph again nodded "yes." He was almost too shocked to speak, and besides, he didn't know what to say.

"After the evening meal?" Jewel suggested. "We shall visit the Child-King after the evening meal."

Joseph retreated inside the house to tell Mary that the caravan had come all the way from Persia to visit their toddler who was the King of the Jews.

That evening, Mary nervously checked everything. She had spent the day fervently preparing to receive guests, sweeping, dusting, and cleaning the white stone house as though the visitors were coming to inspect the facilities.

Young Jesus sat under the meal table playing quietly with a small toy carved by his father. As the twilight faded and the dark streaks crossed the evening sky, the toddler grew tired and he tugged at his mother's robe. Mary supposed the house was as clean as it was going to get. She lit all the candles they had in the house and finally sat down for the first time that evening. Jesus crawled up into his mother's lap and dozed off in her arms.

"THEY'RE COMING!" Joseph heard Melki yelling from down the street. Moments later, there came a rapping at the door. Joseph, opening the door to their visitors, was greeted by the sight of a massive camel outside the house. The driver beat a stick on the camel's knee, and it knelt. The rider looked straight ahead, his finely woven tapestry robe unfurling to the ground as he dismounted. Melchior understood the fine points of greeting royalty. A man must act according to who he is and what people think of him.

At the door, Jewel, who had spoken with Joseph earlier in the day, bowed. "Why did they ride?" Joseph asked. "It's a short distance from your camp."

"Royalty does not walk in dirty streets," Jewel said without superiority or condemnation. He held no personal conviction one way or another as to the cleanliness of Bethlehem pathways. He unrolled a red runner to stretch from the camel to the door of the house. Then Jewel scurried through the door past Joseph with a small chair. He found an appropriate place for his master to sit, returned to the door, and nodded for Melchior to descend.

With the tapestry robe held in one hand, Melchior stepped onto the rug. His Persian features were fixed without expression, his long grey beard finely combed, revealing nothing of his intentions. He walked halfway to the house, then turning, snapped his fingers. Jewel lifted a heavy chest and followed him into the small house. Once Melchior was seated, Jewel at the door nodded, and a second camel was led to the door of the little house. A gaggle of neighbors stood off to the side gawking at the proceedings.

The second camel dislodged Balthazar in the same manner. The third camel did the same with Gaspar, each distinguished rider in equally elegant fashion. Nothing was said or done officially until all three denied kings were seated in front of Mary and the Child.

The small room was tightly packed with three magi and servants. Joseph stood behind his wife. Jesus slept, unimpressed with the finery of the visiting dignitaries.

"We have come to worship the King of the Jews," said Melchior, the first and eldest of the noblemen, speaking in flawless Latin, the official language with just a hint of an accent of Persia. He leaned forward to gaze upon the young Child. Mary brushed back the simple cotton swath that hid Jesus's face. The other two magi leaned forward to see the Babe.

Jesus let out a yawn, and they smiled when they saw the human display of weariness. They didn't know what to expect, but what they expected was not common humanity.

"Why do you call our son King of the Jews?" Joseph demanded with all the humility he could muster. His concern had not faded since the arrival of the foreigners in town that morning.

"We study the stars," Melchior explained. "The stars tell us God has sent a Savior." He said they were called *magi*, or scholars, because their lives were dedicated to studying the scrolls of the ancients.

"How did you know where to find us?" Joseph asked.

Melchior did not answer immediately. He looked from Balthazar's face to Gaspar's countenance, as though asking permission to share a secret.

They nodded.

"We studied copies of the Hebrew scrolls . . . called the holy books of the Jews, the Word of God." Balthazar interrupted, "After reading the Scriptures, we realized God was sending a Child-King to rule the world in peace, that this King will be our Savior."

The magi waited. Joseph stood motionless, uncertain how to respond. He had always believed that God would send Messiah to deliver His people and that Messiah would usher in peace. Every Jewish boy was taught these truths, but these men lived in a land of many gods . . . and many different ways to please the gods. These men came from a land of idols.

What do they want? Joseph thought to himself.

"Your prophet Isaiah promises a Deliverer; He will be born of a virgin and will be called 'Wonderful, Counselor, Mighty God, Everlasting Father, Prince of Peace,' and the government of the world will be on his shoulders," Gaspar explained.

"We believe this to be true," Balthazar spoke up.

Gaspar continued, "Your Scriptures also tell us the Deliverer will be a Savior and we are to call Him Immanuel—God with Us," Gaspar added, because it was from Isaiah, the Scriptures he knew best.

The turbans of the three magi nodded agreement.

"Your Scriptures told us of a star that will be a sign of His birth. When we saw a miraculous star in the sky, we knew it was His star."

Melchior again spoke, his voice quavering with excitement, "We have studied the stars for a long time looking for your Messiah."

"About a year ago," Balthazar interrupted, "a star that had not been in our sky just . . . appeared."

"*His* star," Gaspar insisted.

"This star was brighter than any star we had ever seen. It did not appear in the eastern horizon, as other stars come out at night. This star . . . ."

"*His* star," again interrupted Gaspar.

Melchior continued, "We saw *His* star in the West, while all other stars arise in the East. But no one else saw the star—and we know we saw *His* star—and we knew it would lead us to the Baby-King."

Mary shifted Jesus from one arm to the other. He slept through the conversation, blissfully unaware they were talking about Him. Melchior politely waited for Mary to get comfortable, then continued.

They had prepared gifts for the journey. It was the custom of one king to honor a child born to be king in a neighboring kingdom. The new star told them this was no ordinary king.

"When we arrived in Jerusalem, we went immediately to see the one called Herod the Great to inquire of this Child." Joseph listened carefully as the wise men told of their audience with King Herod. They described Herod as a fat, arrogant, greedy man with food stains on his velvet clothes.

"I AM THE ONLY KING OF THE JEWS!" Herod had blustered at the magi and demanded they tell him where the boy King could be found. "We do not know," was their response. "We only know we saw the star in the western horizon. We came to where the star was revealed to us. We thought you—the king—could tell us where the King of the Jews was born."

Herod consulted with his religious advisors, asking where the Scriptures said this Deliverer would be born. To a man, they answered, "Bethlehem, the City of David."

"Go then," Herod had told the wise men. "Go follow

your star. Find Him and bring me the location . . . I will come to worship the Child with you."

Joseph's brow furrowed. Herod was widely known to be ruthlessly cruel. He had executed his own wife and his children when they threatened his throne. Joseph knew this king was a killer. An unsettling fear lodged in the back of the mind of the young father.

Melchior again spoke, "When we left Jerusalem, we again saw His star. Then *His* star began moving; we followed," the wise man's eyes flashed. "The star moved through the sky—unlike other stars. We obeyed its direction."

Then Melchior clapped his hands for Jewel. A small metal box with cast-iron fittings was placed on the floor before Mary and the sleeping Child. Bending like an old man, Melchior slowly opened the chest. All present saw the light from the candle flames flicker off the pristine gold coins. Then, bending even farther, old Melchior bowed his face to the ground and spread his hands in praise.

"Bless the Lord, O my soul," Melchior prayed in the Hebrew tongue. "Bless the Lord with all that is within me . . . . Bless His holy name."

"These gold coins came from my grandfather Gaumata—12 generations ago—he was the magian-king of Persia. These coins are the venzarena, my inheritance that proves my right to the throne. These coins have been passed from father to son, each son hoping one day to ascend to the throne of Persia. These are my kingly gift for the Child-King."

Every ear in the room strained to hear the words of Melchior. The evening noise of children playing in the afterglow formed a curtain of sound. An insect buzzed at the shut window.

Melchior continued,

"I give these venzarena coins to the Child-King. One day Jesus will rule all of Persia, and my coins will transfer the authority of Persia to Him." Melchior concluded, "In that day, the lion will lie down with the lamb in my Persia."

When Melchior finished worshiping the Child-King, he arose slowly from his knees—the old knees cracked when he got up— and then Melchior stepped back for another magian to worship.

Balthazar, the black magian, then brought an expensive flask filled with frankincense, a rare, aromatic sap, and offered it before the Child. His deep bass voice filled the little house,

"Frankincense is what the priests use in worshiping God, for frankincense opens the heart of God to the worshiper. Your son will be a King-Priest, for He will open the highway for men to worship God."

"Frankincense comes from the commiphora bush that grows in my home land of Ethiopia. Without frankincense, the priests do not worship God. I give to the Priest-King the best symbol of worship that my country can give. May frankincense open the hearts of people everywhere to worship this Child who will be their Priest. And may frankincense move the heart of this Child-Priest to touch them in return."

Then Balthazar fell on his face to offer his frankincense in worship to the Child-Savior.

The third magi—Gaspar—set a cask of myrrh before Mary. The elegant fragrance filled the room with softness. Mary had never experienced a scent so heavenly in her life, even in her trips to Jerusalem.

"This fragrance is for healing," the young Gaspar explained. "It's harvested from the commiphora tree when it is wounded—the tree is bruised for healing." Gaspar did not know that he was predicting that the baby Jesus would die upon a tree for the healing of the nation.

Then Gaspar bowed in worship as had his friends done previously.

"We have read that your Child will be a Savior-King," Gaspar directed his words to both Joseph and Mary. "Your Son will not just deliver Israel from her enemies, nor will He just deliver God's people everywhere from their torments; your Son—this Child-King—will deliver people from their sins."

Gaspar's eyes glowed as he predicted, "Jesus will not just rule from the throne of Israel; He will sit on the throne of people's hearts as their Savior."

After a time, the three magi arose from the floor of the humble dwelling. The oldest glanced to his traveling companions for approval, then he asked,

"May we get a closer look . . .?" His words were unsure; he did not want to impose on the parents. "We've come so far . . . We want to learn His features. One look and we will never forget."

Mary again unfolded the blanket from the Child's face, then smiled warmly at her guests. Then Mary saw it. The wise men had the same eyes as the shepherds. Their adoring eyes were like deep pools of still water, as if this Child had unlocked the mysteries of the ages to them.

1 8

DREAM TO GO HOME A SAFE WAY

....

Protection for the Magi

"Let's camp on this hilltop," Jewel announced to the three magi. They were still in sight of the wall surrounding Bethlehem. A gentle breeze brushed their faces as they unpacked for the night.

The three searching kings hadn't said much since leaving the Babe. All three were in deep thoughts of the Child-King. And they didn't realize it, but the holy child would stay in their thoughts for the rest of their lives. They had seen their Savior and were convinced He was the Promised One.

"When I saw Jesus," Melchior spoke first, "I felt I was looking at the King who would rule the earth. Right there in the small home, I submitted to His reign."

Gaspar had a different response, "When I saw the Child Jesus, I saw God incarnate . . . I saw Immanuel—God With Us." Then Gaspar added, "I worshiped Him."

"I am different from the two of you," Balthazar added to the evening conversation as he took his place at the small fire Jewel had made. "I couldn't forget the prediction of Israel the prophet who said, 'He was wounded for our transgressions, He was bruised for our iniquities . . . All we like sheep have gone astray . . . the Lord has laid on Him the iniquity of us all'" (Isa. 53:5, 6).

Balthazar then added, "I killed a man in Ethiopia, but I was not punished because I was the son of the king. My family could do anything they wanted—we could get away with murder."

Balthazar stopped at the word murder. His eyes drooped as he added, "My government won't punish me, but will God punish me?"

The question wasn't answered. Both Melchior and Gaspar waited for the other to speak, but neither said anything. Then Jewel spoke up,

"The Child we saw was so meek and defenseless. Isaiah predicted the Lord of heaven will lay our sin—your murder—on the Child Jesus, Who will die in your place. You won't have to die."

With that insight, none of the three answered. The magi sat gazing at the stars. It was different looking at the stars from the Holy Land instead of from Persia. The stars seemed higher in the heavens from the west side of the Euphrates River.

"Look . . ." Gaspar pointed to Sagittarius in the eastern sky, "the three band stars are in a straight line. Today is the 25th day of the last month in the year. The three kings are as straight here in Palestine as they were in Persia."

"It was just a year ago we first saw the star in the East," remarked Balthazar. "It was just a year ago that our life was changed. We saw the three kings in a straight line pointing to Orion. Tonight we see it again."

But more than the three kings and Orion, all three had seen His supernatural star—glowing and revolving like shining smoke out of a roaring fire. The smoke turned in upon itself like a wheel within a wheel that kept spinning. No one else saw His star.

Because of the star, they had left their chantry in Persia to travel to the Holy Land. Then the star had led them from Jerusalem to Bethlehem. The star led them to the house where the Child-Jesus was living.

"Will we see the star again tonight?" Balthazar asked.

Neither of the other two answered for they didn't know what to say. Again, Balthazar asked,

"Will we see the star again?"

"Probably not," Melchior answered his question. "The star was to point us to the Messiah; it led us to His very house. Now that we've seen Him and worshiped Him, what else is there to do?" Melchior was turning a page in their book of experiences.

"We might as well go back to tell Herod so he can come worship the Baby-King, just as he asked us to do."

"What will Herod bring to worship the Baby?" Balthazar asked his friends. He was not so much interested in the amount of his offering. Balthazar wanted to know what a reigning king would bring to the Messiah King Who would one day take Herod's place.

"I don't want to tell Herod," Gaspar said to the other magi. "Remember, I was brought up in a palace; I saw treachery in Herod's eyes." Then Gaspar explained, "I saw treachery in the eyes of his court—I don't trust them."

"Who would hurt a baby?" Melchior asked a rhetorical question.

Jewel, who had been listening to the conversation, interrupted, "Let me tell you about Jewish treachery." He pointed down the hill to a dark clump of trees. "That's the place young David led his sheep to drink water when he grew up here in Bethlehem."

"How do you know it was that clump of trees?" Gaspar wanted to analyze Jewel's remark. Jewel did not answer but said,

"I just know."

Gaspar didn't question him any further. Jewel finished his observation, "David was an innocent shepherd boy. Everyone liked him.

"David learned many lessons feeding sheep that prepared him to be the Shepherd-King of Israel. As a shepherd warrior, David killed the giant Goliath. The women sang and danced,

'David killed his ten thousands; Saul has killed his thousands'
(1 Sam. 18:7).

"Saul the king was jealous because David was a threat to
take over his throne. Jewish history tells of many occasions where
Saul tried to kill David. He hurled a javelin at David at a banquet;
later he sent the army to kill David."

Then Jewel paused to draw a conclusion, "Jealousy is a
relentless hunter; jealousy will eat alive anything that usurps its
place."

"What are you telling us, Jewel?" Melchior asked his
servant.

"Herod is a jealous king," Jewel looked deep into
Melchior's eyes without blinking. "King Herod has the throne,
and he will kill anyone who is destined to take his throne."

"We should go back and warn Joseph and Mary,"
Balthazar quickly added.

"No," Gaspar added his wisdom. "If this baby is sent to us
from God—and I think He is Immanuel—then God will take care
of the Child better than we can."

"I must go to that clump of trees to get water," Jewel told
the magi.

Gaspar quickly looked at Jewel as the servant left. It was
a knowing look. Gaspar was doubting if there really was water in
that clump of trees. Jewel never doubted what he said. He grabbed
a skin water bottle and headed down the hillside and later came
back with water.

That night, the three wise men slept around the low
crackling fire. Jewel, who seemed to never need sleep, dozed
throughout the night. When the fire burned low, Jewel fed more
small branches to feed the flames.

The magi were dreaming, and Jewel smiled as though he
knew what they were dreaming.

God appeared to each one separately in a dream. They
awoke abruptly to compare their dreams. God had said the same

thing to each one. They could not doubt in the light what God said in the dark. God said,

"Herod wants to kill the Child-Jesus! Do not go back to Herod. Do not tell Herod where the Child-Jesus is living. Do not go near Jerusalem, for Herod will send his soldiers after you to kill you. Go home around the Dead Sea and return home through the Nabataean Kingdom."

The three magi were suddenly wide awake in the night as those running from a predator. They roused themselves to quickly shake their sleeping blankets. Melchior barked an order into the night,

"Jewel." Then he repeated the name with agitation, "Jewel . . . where are you?"

"I'm putting saddles on the camels," Jewel explained, "We can follow the stars to find our way."

Balthazar offered an excuse, "Couldn't we wait until the morning?" He wanted more sleep, or at least some of Jewel's stimulating tea to arouse him.

"No," Melchior admonished both Balthazar and Gaspar. "We must leave Bethlehem tonight!" Melchior went on to explain, "If the soldiers come looking for us tonight, they will not stop looking in the town of Bethlehem, they will spread out to search for us. Our fire will be seen from a long distance away."

"Pour this water on the red coals," Jewel instructed. "The soldiers must not know that we have been here. Let them think we are somewhere in Jerusalem. They will spend two days looking for us. By that time, we'll be in another kingdom. King Herod can't reach us there."

Within minutes, the magi were astride their camels. Jewel had already packed the supplies and utensils. He wrapped each metal ware with a cloth so they would not rattle. He wanted the caravan to sail like ships, silently through the mountains. No one would see them, and, like ships leaving no trail in its wake, the magi would pass through the area with no evidence of their having been there.

By noon, the caravan passed the Roman tax table at the entrance of the Nabataean kingdom. The Roman centurion stood next to the tax collector to make sure everyone paid their taxes. Unscrupulous tax collectors added to the taxes their own profits. Then to make sure they collected their bloated assessment, they paid off the local centurion; that way, Roman soldiers could be used to collect taxes, with extra coins for the tax collector, and some extra for the pockets of the centurion.

"You men are magi," the centurion observed in the official Latin language. "I can tell by the turbans. The shoes tell me you're from Persia."

The three magi didn't respond. They pretended they didn't understand Latin. But they did. The observations of the centurion scared them. Each magian was smart enough to know that the less the Roman soldiers knew about them, the less they would remember. Perhaps this centurion would send word to Herod that magi entered the Nabataean kingdom.

"They are Roman soldiers," Gaspar spoke the fear of the others. "Herod's Roman soldiers will hunt us down and drag us back to Jerusalem."

"No," said Melchior. "As God will protect the Child-Jesus, He will also protect us. We heard the voice of God in a dream. We are doing what God told us to do. We will be safe."

"God provides a sword for defense," the husky Ethiopian spoke up. He knew the necessity of physical defense. "But we must be wise to know when to keep our sword in its sheath."

"Don't worry," Jewel spoke to the fears of the magi. "I know an old path through the mountains. It's the Arabah Road the Israelites used to come to the Promised Land after 40 years in the wilderness. It was the road through Ammon and Moab; it runs through the border fortresses." Jewel explained how the forts were used before Joshua conquered the land. "These are old Ammonite and Moabite fortresses. No one uses this road because it's hilly, as opposed to the flat Roman road by the Dead Sea and Jordan River. Only local people and shepherds use the hilly road these days."

"How do you know about this road?" Gaspar questioned Jewel.

"Every Jewish boy who studies our history knows this."

Two days later, the three-camel caravan was far beyond the reach of King Herod. The magi began to breathe more easily. They no longer caught themselves looking over their shoulders.

The camels carrying the three magi crossed the border into Syria. Huge Mount Hermon was on their right with its ever-present snowcaps, guiding travelers and assuring everyone of God's faithfulness. The locals called it "the old man of the mountain," the year-round snow caps reminding them of the grey hair on the elderly.

As the evening sky darkened, Balthazar turned to look back, especially peering into the sky. He had done it several times since the evening stars came out. Gaspar wanted to ask about his unusual movement. Was he still afraid of Herod's troops? Gaspar decided to ask when they camped for the night. Then he questioned,

"Why do you keep looking over your shoulder into the sky?"

Balthazar realized that he had been caught. He had been seen looking over his shoulder. He just smiled and said nothing.

"Were you looking for the star?" Gaspar inquired.

Jewel overheard the conversation and added, "His star?"

Again, Balthazar smiled as an indication he had been caught.

"The star will never be seen again," Jewel said. "There are some miracles of God that are never repeated." Then Jewel went on to explain that the Torah teaches God gives some signs for credibility, but they are not repeatable, such as creation and the Jewish people's exit from Egypt when God rolled back the Red Sea. Then Jewel asked,

"Can the Baby-King be born again?"

All shook their heads, "No."

Balthazar agreed with Jewel. "According to my reading of the Torah, the Jews left Egypt only once. They only walked once through the Red Sea on dry land. If a Jew had to cross the Red Sea today, God would not roll back the waters; the Jews would have to use a boat. God's miracles are for His purpose and His time, not for the convenience of His servants."

At that, Melchior interrupted the conversation to ask,

"How then shall we live if we don't have a star to guide us daily?" He went on to explain that life back in the chantry would be different. How would they find out about the Baby-King again? How would they learn about the Baby-King growing into manhood?

"Or the better question," asked Balthazar, "how shall we live in memory of the Baby we saw?"

Gaspar answered, "Past events shape everyone's life, whether it's a marriage, a birth of a baby, or planting of seed in the ground. The experiences of the past, whether we've made commitments, or a vow, or learned a lesson, or we experience failure; those past experiences will influence us forever."

"Does that mean the star will always influence our life?" The wise Melchior asked a question to make people think.

His two friends nodded their heads in approval. Then, Balthazar noted,

"Does it also mean the Baby-King will influence us forever?"

"Just as our life was controlled by the star as we prepared our journey, now we must look back daily on the Baby-King we saw." The Ethiopian's deep voice let out a loud exclamation, "The star will influence me for the rest of my life."

Melchior's response was a benediction, "The Baby-King will influence me for the rest of my life."

Jewel had been listening intently to the conversation. He understood people better than most humans, but he understood the magi best. That was his life's journey. The darkening shadows of the evening hid his smile. Jewel was pleased with what he heard, knowing that the Father in heaven was also pleased, so he was constrained to add,

"The star was in our experience, so it will guide everything we do tomorrow, and all other tomorrows beyond that." The three wise men nodded. "But what we read in the holy book—whether the Pentateuch, Psalms, or Isaiah—is a written remembrance of what God has done in the past for others. We can learn from their memory or from the Baby-King we worshiped. Because of that Child, we can serve the Lord so much better."

Jewel made the point that the Scriptures will guide their lives, just as God's intervention—the star—guided them to the Baby-King. We must not focus our life on the things God uses in our experience—the star—but we must focus our life on the thing the star pointed out—the Baby-King.

1 9

JOSEPH'S DREAM OF DANGER
AND TRIP TO EGYPT

....

God's Watch-Care

Mary and Jesus slept peacefully in their small home. The little town of Bethlehem dozed beneath a silent blanket of stars. A dog barked in the distance, then let out a lonesome whimper. Joseph was awake, but it was not the dog that had roused him, nor was it his concern for the safety of the expensive gifts the unusual visitors had brought to Jesus. A fearful shadow stood in the back of his mind. Something was terribly wrong. Joseph had been startled out of his sleep, frightened by a dream.

He dreamed he was working in the shop . . . working on a table. Joseph, a skilled carpenter, was growing frustrated with his seeming inability to balance the table's legs, so he set it aside. Instead, Joseph saw himself in the dream putting the finishing touches on a cradle he had fashioned for the royal family. He stood back to admire his handiwork and realized he had mistakenly made not a cradle but a feed trough, a manger. Then terror gripped his heart as a long dark shadow from the door fell across the trough. Had the king come for his cradle? Would the king be angry because a manger was built for him and not a magnificent cradle?

Joseph turned to greet a visitor in the doorway, but it was not the king who had entered the shop. There stood a familiar figure—an angel—towered above everything in the room. Joseph was certain he had seen this person before.

"Get up, Joseph," the angel warned. "Danger lies on the other side of dawn." Joseph knew this voice, but from where?

"An enemy is coming to kill the Child."

Then Joseph knew. This was the messenger from God who had foretold the birth of Jesus. Joseph stood stunned, almost afraid to move. He didn't know what to do. He stared at the angel wide-eyed.

"Hurry, " the angel warned. "There is no time. Death comes after sunup. "

Herod! Joseph knew immediately the angel spoke of King Herod. He thought, *That heartless killer is coming for my Child.*

"Go to Egypt. Take the child and his mother and stay in Egypt until I tell you," the angel said. Joseph bowed his head and nodded his willingness to obey.

"Leave now," was the angel's final warning.

There was a faint light in the eastern sky when Joseph led Mary out to the donkey. He helped her up then brought her the bundled Child. He threw two sacks filled with gold, frankincense and myrrh over the animal, then tied them securely.

"We'll have money to live in Egypt," he said, patting the treasure sacks. He knew their contents but hoped everyone else would think the sacks were filled with utensils for cooking.

The animal's hoofs clicked on the stones as they left their home. When the donkey halted to feel his way in the dark shadows, Joseph urgently pulled on the reins,

"Hurry," he pleaded. By the time they made their way out of Bethlehem, the light in the east had grown bold enough to reveal the dark trees and stone walls that lined the road, though sunrise was still at least an hour away.

A few miles out of Bethlehem, the donkey refused to go any farther, jerking his head angrily against Joseph's direction.

The donkey pulled Joseph toward a little stream at the side of the road.

"What's wrong?" Mary was concerned.

"He smells the creek water," Joseph explained. "We left so quickly I didn't give him water."

Mary decided it was a good time to feed Jesus and found a secluded spot out of the breeze among some rocks. Joseph led the animal into the stream to drink. Moments later, he heard shouts coming from the direction of Jerusalem. Then Joseph heard the unmistakable tramp of Roman soldiers. These soldiers were not aimlessly strolling toward Bethlehem. Joseph heard the clamor of full-battle march.

He pulled the animal down the creek into some bushes and prayed the donkey would not let out a bray in protest.

"I hear them," Mary whispered to Joseph.

"Stay hidden in the rocks," Joseph instructed his wife.

The troops were led by a centurion dressed in battle gear, proudly astride his prancing white steed. Spotting the stream, he stopped to give his horse a drink, signaling the troops to continue their sonorous march. The horse waded into the shallow water near the rocks where mother and child were hidden. The centurion leaned back in his saddle and patted the rump of his horse.

Mary silently prayed, *"Lord, don't let Jesus cry."* The toddler closed His eyes and slept.

The horse turned around in the stream, looking for firm footing amid the slippery rocks. In the darkness before the dawn, the Roman officer couldn't see into the bushes where Joseph hid with the donkey, but Joseph could see the centurion clearly enough. Joseph saw angry eyes staring back at him. He wanted to run but held his ground. Escape was impossible, for the battle-hardened horse would certainly outrun him. And even though the distraction might enable Mary and Jesus to get away undetected, the angel had instructed Joseph to take his wife and child to Egypt, so he was determined to remain hidden.

The donkey swished its tail, and Joseph prayed, *Please don't let the donkey give me away.* The donkey stood silently.

Suddenly, the centurion jerked at his reins, and the white horse ascended the bank from the stream and took up its trot beside the procession of soldiers. One hundred soldiers marched steely-eyed. They looked neither to their right or left. With hands on their swords and death on their minds, they marched on toward Bethlehem.

Quickly, Joseph and Mary were back on the road. Now Joseph picked up his pace, heading for Egypt. By mid-morning, they had traveled far enough from Bethlehem that their fears slowly subsided. The sun washed away the dread of the night. The more babies and small children they saw along the way, the safer they felt.

Three nights later, they were halfway to Egypt. Everything in sight was different from their hometown of Nazareth. Back in Galilee, the homes were built out of white fieldstone; as they drew nearer to Egypt, the houses were made of clay, their dirty lime painted walls caked from the sun. Uncomfortable with the local accommodations and thinking it would be best to keep his family from the prying eyes of the opportunistic local authorities, Joseph stopped for the night at an oasis. The young family rested among strangers under the tall royal palms. They were almost ready to go to sleep when a gruff voice was heard complaining from the other side of the oasis.

The burly new arrival dropped his pack. Sticking his aching feet, sandals and all, into the cool water, he complained to anyone who would listen of walking all day. A few mumbled in agreement, but neither Joseph nor Mary said a word.

"I never want to see another Jew!" the boisterous voice carried over the water to Mary and Joseph. "Those crazy Jews kill each other." This remark was met with silence, though a few nods were exchanged.

"Yesterday," he bellowed, "King Herod killed all the

baby boys in Bethlehem!" The traveler went on to describe in graphic detail how the Roman soldiers had stacked the bodies of the babies near the well in Bethlehem. The word on the streets of Jerusalem was that Herod had ordered the death of all male children two years old and younger because of a rumor that a rival to his throne had been born in Bethlehem.

"Herod, a Jew himself, sent a hundred soldiers to slaughter all the babies and any parents who got in their way. Terrible!" The agitated traveler swore again at the Jews. "I never want to go back there."

Mary looked at Joseph through the evening shadows; he returned a knowing glance. She silently wondered, *Why was our Jesus saved . . . and all those little boys slaughtered?*

She looked at Jesus sleeping in her arms and whispered to Him, "Remember always, God loves You and will protect You."

Joseph and Mary stayed in Egypt for approximately two years. Then an angel spoke to Joseph in a dream, telling him to return. The couple brought the Child-Jesus back to Nazareth, where He grew into manhood.

WHAT THEN SHALL WE DO WITH THE BABY-KING?

....

His Coming Changed Them Internally

The three magi and Jewel entered Narhet, the home village of Melchior from which they had launched their journey. Nothing had changed. No new houses were constructed, no new people; everyone looked the same as they did a year earlier. The camels stopped by the city well for water. Melchior gazed out over his neighborhood,

"Nothing changes . . . and life repeats itself . . . all of life is a circle."

Jesus the Baby-King had been born; they gave him kingly gifts and worshiped him. The guard house was still dirty and unkempt. But Commander was nowhere to be seen. Soldiers were sleeping in the shade, seeking protection from the scorching sun. Is this the peace promised by the Baby-King who would deliver mankind? Melchior thought a king of peace would bring peace. But nothing changed.

Leading his camel by the stirrups, Melchior walked up the hill toward the chantry.

The chantry had not changed, thought Melchior. Then he announced to his small party, "The first thing I want to do is go to the Circle Room and check the maps. I want to remember every star in its place and the heavenly bodies as God made them." Then quickly added, "I'll check into the circle room tonight to see if there is any further evidence of the miraculous star."

"His star," replied Jewel.

"Ha . . . ha . . . ha," Balthazar laughed out loud. "I'm not as intellectual as you. The first thing I want to do is find a bed and sleep with my own blanket."

Then Melchior interrupted,

"After checking the charts in the Circle Room, I shall walk all the way around the chantry," he commented. "It's more than a house; the chantry is my life, and my spirit lives in every room."

"That's what we expect of the Circle Maker!" Jewel laughed.

Gaspar could not be left out, "The first thing I shall do is find a warm bath and sleep in its soap suds before the evening meal."

Jewel had been listening to their wishes, but he also had a passion.

"The first thing I shall do is to pick new tea leaves from the well and then brew some hot water for tea." Then Jewel wiped the trail dust from his face and commented on the request by Gaspar for a hot bath. "I shall prepare three warm baths; it shall take a few minutes to get the water warm. Then after your naps, I shall meet you in the patio under the fig tree for some hot tea."

First Evening Home Under the Fig Tree

"Gentlemen, we're home. What do we do now?" Melchior, the aged Persian magian, began the evening conversation. A simple question, yet the profound implication stumped the three magi. They looked at one another without answering, each deep within his own thoughts.

Melchior continued, "Narhet is the same. The Baby-King was born and nothing happened. Is He the King who will rule the earth? There is no symbol of divine law in our village. The governor still rules our providence, and the king still rules our nation . . ."

Gaspar interrupted, "If we told the governor and the king . . . maybe they will go worship the Child-King."

"No," the booming voice of Balthazar commanded the room. "The baby is not yet King; He's only a child." He then asked, "Must we wait till the baby grows up to have His peace ushered in?"

Then Jewel entered the conversation, which was an unusual thing for a servant. But they could not reject Jewel's wisdom,

"Since the baby is the Messiah-King, the sacred writings of Israel suggest He will do miracles. That means He must grow into manhood. His Kingdom may not come for 30 years. So, let's wait for reports from the Holy Land. Let's see if we hear about His miracles. Everyone will talk about it, and travelers coming this way will tell us if God is with Him and what He will do to bring peace."

"Oh, no," Balthazar moaned. "Thirty years is a long time. What will happen to us during that time?" the Ethiopian pondered what would happen to him—to them—as they waited for the Child-King to introduce His Kingdom. "What are we going to do during the 30 years while we wait for the child to grow into manhood?" Then Balthazar added, "We may die before He rules the world."

Jewel suggested, "We can study the Jewish Scriptures to find everything about the Messiah-King that is written there." Jewel told them to start reading and memorizing Scripture. Then discuss among themselves to learn as much about the Baby-King as possible.

"Since He is the King who will set up a kingdom of peace, then we must study the Holy writings to learn about life in His Kingdom. We must prepare ourselves for a reign of peace . . ."

Melchior commented, "Where the lion shall lie down with the lamb."

Balthazar added, "Where the curse will be lifted from the land."

"But the part of the Kingdom that I look for," added Gaspar, "is peace among fighting nations when they shall beat their swords into ploughshares, and their spears into pruning hooks."

The three magi talked long after the twilight faded into darkness. They walked out past the perimeters of the shimmering olive oil lamps into the darkness. They smiled as they searched the starry night.

"We shall see the three kings and Orion perfectly aligned again next year."

"If we are the three kings," asked Balthazar, "is Orion Jewel?"

"Oh, no!" They heard Jewel's voice from the darkness. "Orion is Jesus, the Baby- King. Just as you worshiped the child, so the three stars point perfectly to Orion on December 25th."

"We shall study the Scriptures, and the stars," Melchior added. "Yes, we shall see the multitude of stars as great as the multitude of the sons of Abraham, just as God promised him long ago."

First Morning Home

The sun had come up an hour ago, and Melchior was still in the bed. He stretched his tired muscles from the long trip to Bethlehem and felt good that he had accomplished his dream. He had worshiped the Baby-King and knew that he had pleased God in heaven. Then he thought,

Where's Jewel? Jewel had usually awakened him at this time. There was no hot tea by his bed. He listened for sounds of bumping utensils from the kitchen area, but heard nothing. He walked the entire circular hallway around the inside of the house, calling,

"Jewel . . . Jewel . . ." There was no answer.

Jewel was not at the well, nor at the patio under the fig tree; he was nowhere to be seen. *Has he gone to the market?* Melchior thought perhaps Jewel would return shortly.

When Gaspar entered the kitchen, he also asked, "Where is Jewel?" The two men then talked about small matters from their journey, nothing important. Finally, Balthazar entered the room to ask the same question,

"Where's Jewel?"

Melchior was the most puzzled of the three, thinking to himself,

Jewel has never disappeared; he's always been here when I needed him.

When the sun reached the height of the heavens—noon—Melchior walked into town looking for Jewel, but he was not at the market. He asked several if anyone had seen Jewel. None had seen him.

That evening, Melchior prepared the food; he kept asking, "Where's the dish . . . where's the spoon . . . where does he keep the bread?" The three magi were lost without Jewel.

The winter's wind blew sand under the door, and Melchior swept the hallway. Gaspar drew water from the well, and Balthazar struggled to get the fire going, thinking, *A few breaths from Jewel and flames would dance—but not me.*

Questions about Jewel dominated the evening meal. How could a man who had been so faithful disappear; where could he be?

"Did he return to Bethlehem to worship the Baby-King?"

"Did he want his freedom, so he just ran away?"

"Did he desire serving a rich man, so he returned to Flavius?"

"Was he sent to help us find the star, and since our journey is complete, he's not needed?"

Then finally Melchior concluded,

"Jewel is a rational man; he's as wise as a magian. If he's alive, he knows what he is doing and if he's controlling his life. He shall return if he chooses."

Then Gaspar added his comments,

"I have read the Pentateuch, Psalms, and Isaiah. I have learned how God guides the affairs of his servants on this earth. He uses angels; maybe Jewel was an angel, and he was sent to us by God, but we were unaware . . . ."

"Be not forgetful to entertain strangers: for thereby some have entertained angels unawares"
(Hebrews 13:2, *KJV*)

2 1

FINDING MYTHS
AMONG THE TRUTHS

···

An Accurate Twenty-first Century Assessment
of the Three Kings

Dr. Legna Lewej, a Ph.D. in archaeology from the Middle
East, is prepared to lecture students at Liberty University on the
facts and fictions of *The Three Searching Kings: Following the Star to
Bethlehem.** Dr. Lewej enters Towns Auditorium on the university
campus. Students have been assigned to read *The Three Searching
Kings: Following the Star to Bethlehem.* Dr. Lewej opens class
with prayer and then makes the following comments: "There are
many Bible truths found in the historical novel you have just read.
However, with all historical novels, the author has taken the liberty
to interpret scenes that are hypothetical, yet in the author's mind
these scenes might have existed. The author also creates narratives
of people speaking, not because he knows the speech of them, but
because it is what the actors in the historical novel may have said.

Dr. Lewej says to the class, "Here are a few of the facts
that we know are true according to the Bible. Let's begin with the
truth":

- Magi came from the East (probably Persia, but we don't
  know for sure).
- Magi brought three gifts: gold, frankincense, and myrrh.
- Magi are searching for the One who is born "King of the

Jews." (We asked the question how did they know He was King of the Jews).

- There was a star that they saw back in Persia, and they followed the star to Bethlehem.
- For reasons unknown to us, their intent was to worship the newborn King.
- Apparently, the star appeared intermittently; it led them to Jerusalem. They had to ask questions, then the star led them to Bethlehem and stood over the house where the child, Jesus, was living.
- All of Jerusalem and King Herod were "troubled" at the search of the three kings. Can we assume that they went throughout the city asking directions for the place of the birth of the King Baby?
- Members of the religious community knew the Scriptures that said that the Jewish Messiah was to be born in Bethlehem. King Herod did not go to Bethlehem but sent the magi to find directions to the Child King, and report to him.
- When the magi arrived at the house, Jesus was no longer a babe in arms (*brethos*, Luke 2:16), but they found a child (*baidion*, Matt. 2:8).
- The wise men were warned by God in a dream not to tell Herod, so they went home another way (presumably around the east side of the Dead Sea, rather than returning through Jerusalem).
- Joseph the father was warned by the angel of the Lord in a dream to take Mary and Jesus and hide in Egypt because people were going to try to kill Jesus.
- Joseph quickly left Bethlehem and went to Egypt and remained there until Herod died.

After listing the facts, Dr. Lewej told the students that some of the following were based on tradition but not necessarily based on biblical text. He pointed out that, "Tradition may be true, or tradition may be false, but many times tradition contains

both half-truths and half error." Then Dr. Lewej pointed out the
following:

The following may not be true:

- There may be more than three kings—some biblical scholars
  say perhaps as many as one hundred—because all Jerusalem
  was "troubled" over their appearance in the city.
- Magi came from Persia.
- Magi represented the three main divisions of humanity as
  seen in the sons of Noah.
- The names of the alleged three magi.
- The fact that the magi were kings and were those in line for a
  crown of a nation or people group.

Now Professor Lewej pointed out to the students the
places where the Scriptures concerning the magi were found. He
asked them to read carefully the following Scripture.

> *¹Jesus was born in Bethlehem in Judea, during the reign of King
> Herod. About that time some wise men from eastern lands
> arrived in Jerusalem, asking,*
> *²"Where is the newborn king of the Jews? We saw his star as it
> rose, and we have come to worship him."*
> *³King Herod was deeply disturbed when he heard this, as was
> everyone in Jerusalem.*
> *⁴He called a meeting of the leading priests and teachers of religious
> law and asked, "Where is the Messiah supposed to be born?"*
> *⁵"In Bethlehem in Judea," they said, "for this is what the prophet
> wrote:*
> *⁶'And you, O Bethlehem in the land of Judah, are not least among
> the ruling cities of Judah, for a ruler will come from you who will
> be the shepherd for my people Israel.'"*
> *⁷Then Herod called for a private meeting with the wise men, and
> he learned from them the time when the star first appeared.*

⁸Then he told them, "Go to Bethlehem and search carefully for the child. And when you find him, come back and tell me so that I can go and worship him, too!" ⁹After this interview the wise men went their way. And the star they had seen in the east guided them to Bethlehem. It went ahead of them and stopped over the place where the child was.

¹⁰When they saw the star, they were filled with joy!

¹¹They entered the house and saw the child with his mother, Mary, and they bowed down and worshiped him. Then they opened their treasure chests and gave him gifts of gold, frankincense, and myrrh.

¹²When it was time to leave, they returned to their own country by another route, for God had warned them in a dream not to return to Herod.

¹³After the wise men were gone, an angel of the Lord appeared to Joseph in a dream. "Get up! Flee to Egypt with the child and his mother," the angel said. "Stay there until I tell you to return, because Herod is going to search for the child to kill him."

¹⁴That night Joseph left for Egypt with the child and Mary, his mother,

¹⁵and they stayed there until Herod's death. This fulfilled what the Lord had spoken through the prophet: "I called my Son out of Egypt"

(Matt. 2:1-15, NLT).

Professor Lewej then pointed out that he would like to add to what we know about the tradition involving the three magi. First, tradition tells us that Thomas the apostle came to their home and baptized them in Christian baptism.

Next, Dr. Lewej discussed the tradition of the death of the magi. "The three magi met together on a hill near their home, and they pledged to each other to build a tomb so they would be buried together. They planned to meet in that site every year to renew their vow. They celebrated communion on Christmas day, 54 A.D. and soon thereafter died. Melchior was the first to die on January 1st at the age of 116, Balthazar died on the 6th day of January at age 112 and Casper died on the 11th day of January at age 109."

The next major tradition involves the mother of Constantine, the Roman Caesar (circa 274-337). His mother, Empress St. Helena (circa 248-330) supposedly discovered their bodies in Persia in 325 A.D. Helena was on a pilgrimage to the Holy Land to find and designate the various holy sites. Most historians think that she relied on local tradition (almost 300 years old at the time) to designate certain cites. Many times, she was wrong. Whether Helena was right about the three magi is not known. Helena took the remains of the three magi to Constantinople (the city later renamed Istanbul) in one chest and buried them together in the church of St. Sophia, in the city named for her son.

Tradition tells us that Emperor Constantine I (circa 288-337) took the remains of the three wise man in a huge sarcophagus (a stone coffin that is carved ornately) to Milan, Italy, as a gift to the city. The stone coffin was loaded onto a wooden cart and pulled into the city by a team of oxen. The cart entered the city through Porta Ticinese; it sank in the mud. The Bishop of Milan, Eustortio, who was receiving the sarcophagus, determined that the accident was a sign from God. He built the first basilica in that city on that site.

The next thing we know about the three magi is that the Holy Roman Emperor Friedrich I, called Barbarossa in 1163 A.D., gave the stone coffin to Cologne, Germany, as a special gift looted from Milan when he conquered the city in March, 1162. He gave to Cologne the bones of the three wise men. It is said their remains were transported to Cologne by three ships (source of the Christmas carol, *I Saw Three Ships on Christmas Day*).

The historical record of the bones carried from Persia to Constantinople to Milan to Cologne is all based on tradition. Perhaps the bones never left Persia; Helena is not known as an accurate researcher. Perhaps something else happened to the remains of the three wise men.

Marco Polo wrote that he was shown the three tombs of the wise men at Saveh, south of Tehran, in 1270 A.D. Polo wrote, "The bodies are still intact with hair and beard remaining."

Dr. Lewej speculated to the class, "Which tradition is right . . .?"

Dr. Lewej was quick to tell the class that Europe was filled with churches that claimed to have artifacts from the life and ministry of Jesus Christ. There are churches that claim to have splinters of the cross, the crown of thorns, and the shroud that covered the body of Jesus. Also, we would speculate that churches wanting to claim importance would claim to have other artifacts from the life of Jesus such as the bones of the three wise men.

Dr. Lewej suggested,

"I believe God allowed all of the artifacts to disappear. If the artifacts were real, worshipers would put great credibility in the artifacts; probably more faith in things than in the God of the Bible or even the Bible itself."

Dr. Lewej summarized to the class, "All stories about the wise men contain some truth and some traditional fiction. There is little truth in fiction; it is only written to entertain us. But there's also a little fiction in truth; it is written to inform us.

So all the facts about the three kings may have some truth, just like the story created by Elmer Towns may have some truth. If it has enough truth to make you believe it could have happened, and you enjoy the story, then the author has accomplished his purpose.

If the story has made you doubt whether it happened the way it's described, that's all well and true. But remember, the historical fiction of the three searching who followed the star to Bethlehem directs your attention to the eternal values to which it points. Before the story of the three magi should make you forget things in your life that never happened, remember the three searching kings never became kings on this earth. Perhaps some of you have great dreams and you will never accomplish your dreams. But just as the dreams of the three searching kings drove them a lifetime, let your dreams be your motivation for a lifetime.

Also remember that dreams are powerful. They can motivate you to face sacrifice, danger, and overcome prejudice related to past traditions. Dreams can bring cultures together and people of different color together, just as the dream of the three wise men brought them into one common journey. If your dreams can overcome prejudice and past traditions and give you a meaningful journey in life, all well and good.

So let's go to the end of the story. The three magi pursued the dreams until they arrived at the Christ Child who was the King of the Jews. They worshiped Him, and thereafter they served the king that they worshiped. And in so doing, they thereafter attained kingly qualities, which is one reason they are called *Three Searching Kings.*

....

Go Help Them Understand

"JEWEL . . ." God yelled from His throne. God wasn't looking for His angel named Jewel; God knows everything, so He knew where Jewel was located. Jewel was not lost. God was calling for Jewel's benefit.

"Jewel . . . come here!"

Jewel was to be assigned as aguardian angel to Old Testament scholars who knew a few things about the prediction of the coming Messiah. Jewel was to help blend what each Magian knew with the other two, so together they could search for the Baby born in Bethlehem.

Angels are not omniscient; they don't know everything. They learn just as humans on earth learn things. Jewel will learn many things as he guides the three magi toward their goal of finding the One born King of the Jews.

Jewel came dashing through the annals of heaven to the very throne room where God's presence was manifested. Jewel knew that God was everywhere and that God saw all he did, but he also knew God had a localized presence where He sat on His throne.

"Holy . . . Holy . . . Holy . . ." Jewel heard the seraphim singing praises to God as he entered the throne room. Under his breath, Jewel joined them,

"Holy . . . Holy . . . Holy . . . ." What else could one utter in the presence of righteous perfection?

Jewel hid his face, for he couldn't look on God, for God is Spirit. Jewel didn't even try to sneak a peek for he knew he couldn't see God, for there's no physical person to see. God is a Spirit and invisible. Beyond that, gazing on God is prohibited.

With head bowed in worship, Jewel approached the throne, awaiting orders from the God of the Universe. He had never been summoned into God's presence, nor had he ever been given a special divine task. God spoke:

"Jewel, I want you to help three men who are studying the Scriptures. Help these three understand that My Son is coming to earth. These three men have a special place to announce to mankind that My only begotten Son will be born of a virgin."

God communicated thought to thought, so automatically Jewel knew the names of the three magi and where they were located.

"Remember," God said, "help them understand the Scriptures about My Son. Then help them find their way to Bethlehem where He will be born. These three will perform kingly functions. Just as earthly kings born in one kingdom send gifts to kings in other kingdoms, I want these three to worship My Son with kingly gifts.

Jewel answered God, "But suppose they will not be submissive to help prepare for the coming of Your Son?"

"They will," God answered, reminding Jewel his task was to help these men understand the Scriptures and to lead them. "When these three men understand the awesome event that My Son will be born among them, they will do everything possible to go where I send them, and do what I tell them to do."

"Jewel," God told His angel, "your job is one of the most important tasks to prepare the world for My Son. Can you do it?"

"Yes."

Jewel left the presence of God with awe and dread. He knew where he was going—to Persia. He knew the men whom he was to help—Melchior, Balthazar, and Gaspar. He knew his task: to guide them in their understanding of Scriptures about the Son of God coming to earth. Then he was to guide them to Bethlehem to offer the Babe kingly gifts. Jewel also knew he couldn't reveal his nature to the three magi because angels are "entertained unawares" (Heb. 13:2) by God's children on earth.

Elmer Towns who has won awards for fiction, Bible study, and theological research. He has written a dozen best-selling books in various fields. He writes this historical novel about three magi who searched for the Baby-King of the Jews so they can bring the child kingly gifts. These three magi-denied kings are prepared to help announce to the world the One born "King of the Jews."

The lives of Melchior, Balthazar and Gasper are drawn from research into early church legend and tradition. Many facets of their actions are true because they are drawn from the gospel of Matthew. So page after page uncovers the dreams of three kings, rejected from earthly thrones, who ultimately offer kingly gifts at the birth of "the King of the Jews."

Suspense awaits at each new event. What is the mystery of the Circle Room? Why does Jewel know so much? Was the star just an unusually bright star, or a supernatural appearance? How will each magian face human temptation and overcome them to make his way to Bethlehem? Finally, how will worshiping the Baby-King change their lives?